P9-AGT-962

STRANGER
DANGER

STRANGER DANGER

MAREN STOFFELS

TRANSLATED BY LAURA WATKINSON

UNDERLINED

This is a work of fiction. Names, characters, places, and incidents either are the product of the author's imagination or are used fictitiously. Any resemblance to actual persons, living or dead, events, or locales is entirely coincidental.

Text copyright © 2021 by Maren Stoffels
Cover art copyright © 2023 by Visualspectrum/Stocksy
Translation copyright © 2023 by Laura Watkinson

All rights reserved. Published in the United States by Underlined, an imprint of Random House Children's Books, a division of Penguin Random House LLC, New York. Originally published in paperback by Leopold, Amsterdam, in 2021.

Underlined is a registered trademark and the colophon is a trademark of Penguin Random House LLC.

GetUnderlined.com

Educators and librarians, for a variety of teaching tools,
visit us at RHTeachersLibrarians.com

Library of Congress Cataloging-in-Publication Data is available upon request.
ISBN 978-0-593-64744-8 (pbk.) — ISBN 978-0-593-64745-5 (ebook)

The text of this book is set in 10.5-point Scala.
Interior design by Ken Crossland

Printed in the United States of America
1st Printing
First American Edition

Random House Children's Books supports the First Amendment
and celebrates the right to read.

Penguin Random House LLC supports copyright. Copyright fuels creativity, encourages diverse voices, promotes free speech, and creates a vibrant culture. Thank you for buying an authorized edition of this book and for complying with copyright laws by not reproducing, scanning, or distributing any part in any form without permission. You are supporting writers and allowing Penguin Random House to publish books for every reader.

For the little miracle inside my belly,

who grew bigger as I was writing: Lovas.

SUMMER

I walked across the schoolyard, clutching my bag.

The textbooks banged against my hip with every step.

OAKWOOD HIGH SCHOOL

Had the building looked this big online?

I needed to stay calm—they can smell fear.

I put a toffee in my mouth.

The sweetness made me feel a little calmer.

"Hey, it's your first day, right?"

The man coming toward me looked like he was in his early thirties.

He was dressed neatly, but his sneakers were all scuffed up.

"I'm Reid Hunter, the head of the biology department

here. Come with me, and I can introduce you to your new class."

My new class . . .

Any minute now, I'd be seeing the real-life versions of the online profile pics I'd studied so closely this summer.

"Mr. Hunter!" A boy gave him a friendly slap on the shoulder.

Even before Reid Hunter said the boy's name, I knew who he was.

"Vin! Good to see you here on time, man."

It was like Reid Hunter and I were parting the waters. All the students stepped aside for us.

As long as this man was here, clearly nothing bad could happen to me.

But what about later, when I had to do it all on my own?

LOTUS

The streetlights cast patches of yellow on the path through the trees. Spot drags me along, as if he hasn't been outside for weeks. As he pulls the leash tight for the umpteenth time, I burst out laughing.

"Hey, take it easy, Spot!"

I'm following my usual route, through the woods, and then across the bridge and back home. The place is deserted, as it always is around this time. I love going out late at night. Feels like I'm all alone in the world for a while.

Something rustles in the bushes. Spot tugs at the leash, but in the opposite direction this time, which is weird. He usually runs after every bird or squirrel, so it must be something else.

I pause for a moment and hear it again.

"Hello?" My voice sounds unnaturally loud in the darkness.

There's no answer. Of course not. Nothing ever happens here.

I walk with Spot toward the big clearing and take my phone from my pocket. Even this prehistoric cell phone, which belongs to my dad, is going to be forbidden soon. Nova came up with the idea of having a complete lockdown so we can focus on our exams. So typical of her, coming up with something like that. And renting a remote farmhouse for a week.

I have no idea where we're going because Nova refuses to tell us. She wants it to be a surprise.

Just the thought of the next week is making me nervous. If it were only the two of us, it'd be cool, but now that Vin's coming, everything's different. He might be great at lying to Nova, but that doesn't mean I am too.

Maybe I should have said I didn't want to go, but then Nova would have started asking questions. And my best friend does not take no for an answer.

I flip open the cell. This isn't my usual phone; it's an extra phone, especially for him. It was my idea, just to be on the safe side. If Nova ever goes snooping around in my messages, she won't find anything.

Nova . . . I feel nauseous again at the thought of her ever finding out.

Some days it's like Nova can see everything that's going on inside me. Like my skin is made of Saran wrap and she can look all the way through me.

My thumb hovers over the send button. I know what I need to say. The sentence is ready.

How's he going to react?

Do I really want to do this?

Spot barks impatiently, as if he's trying to tell me I have to go through with it.

"You're right," I say quietly, and I press send.

> We need to stop doing this.
> It's getting too dangerous. x

When we reach the clearing, Spot squats down. I dig around in my pocket for a plastic bag.

"What do you think?" I ask Spot. "Did I make a dumb decision?"

Nova hates when I talk to Spot like he's a person, but it's automatic. Maybe because I can't talk to anyone else about this.

"Think he's going to be mad at me?"

I bend down to pick up the poop. When I stand up, I see something on the other side of the clearing. Someone's standing in front of the bridge, exactly where I need to go.

In the five years I've been walking Spot here at this time of night, I've never met another dog owner.

But then I realize there's no dog. It's someone on their own.

Am I seeing this right? Or are they just standing still?

A shock goes through me. Are they watching me?

Yes, I can see it clearly now. They're looking my way.

Spot has noticed them, too, and he starts growling quietly. He never does that. He's always happy to see people.

What's going on? What do they want from me?

"What a creep," I whisper as, for the first time in five years, I turn around and change my route. "Come on, Spot. Let's go this way."

I don't see anything out of the ordinary outside my house—the street is as quiet as ever.

Why did that person freak me out so much? It was just someone out for a late-night walk, someone like me who can't get to sleep before midnight.

As I put my key in the lock, there's a buzz in my pocket. Has he already sent a reply?

Leaving the key in the front door, I take out my phone. I don't recognize the number on the screen.

That's strange. . . . There's only one person who knows this number.

When I click on the envelope symbol, the text message appears.

I stare at the words on the screen:

I know what you're up to.

Don't forget: buy dog treats.
  Or that animal could cause problems.

LOTUS

"Hurry up!" Outside, there's impatient honking. "Your taxi's here!"

Standing in the hallway, I clutch my extra phone. Leaving behind my own phone isn't a problem, but this one? I must have called the unknown number seven times last night and this morning, but no one answered. No voice mail, nothing. Like trying to contact a ghost.

I know what you're up to.

That is my worst fear: someone finding out. I was always so careful, but now someone has discovered my secret.

I put a stop to it, but what if everything still comes out?

Upstairs, Warner turns off his music. "Lotus, have you left yet?"

"Almost," I shout to my brother.

"Hey, have fun!" The music goes back on.

I want to leave my phone on the cabinet in the hall, but they're like two repelling magnets. I can't put it down.

More honking from outside, followed by Nova's voice. "Lotus!"

Spot whines impatiently and tugs at the leash.

"Yeah, yeah, we're going."

I slip my phone into the front pocket of my bag.

"Hit the gas, Romes!"

Romy drives out of the street. Nova's sister is a couple of years older than us and offered to drop us off on her way to some music festival, having just got her driver's license. You wouldn't know it, though, because she peels off like she's been a race car driver for years. I'm already nauseous before we've left the street.

A man furiously waves at us to slow down, but Romy just sticks up her middle finger in response.

"Killjoy."

At the highway on-ramp, she hits the gas hard again. I peek at her in the rearview mirror and remember why I'm always a bit scared of her. Her dark makeup makes her look kind of sinister.

Nova imitates everything her big sister does. Her hair is dyed gray, and she wears these big black shoes, which are now kicked off next to her feet.

"You okay?" says Vin beside me. His voice is low, with a hoarse edge to it.

I smile as he tries to peer around Nova's big suitcase. It's on his lap because there was no room in the trunk. My bag is between us, and Spot is lying on the mat by Nova's shoes.

"Fine," I say.

"You're kind of green," Vin says, giving me a worried look. "Are you carsick?"

I nod.

"Try opening the window. It helps."

When I wind the window down a bit, fresh air flows into the car. I hold my nose to the gap and take a deep breath. He's right—it works.

I really want to check my phone, but I can't. Not here, crammed in the car with three other people.

Has another message arrived? I don't understand how Unknown got my number. There's only one person who has it, isn't there?

"How far do we have to drive?" I ask.

Nova looks back, grinning. "Nice try, but it's still a surprise."

Romy turns on the radio, and Nova drums along on her bare legs. It's still chilly outside, but as soon as winter's over, Nova always dresses like it's the height of summer. Her fraying jeans are cut off mid-thigh. Her legs are tanned and lean.

I see a new gold chain around her ankle. I bet Vin gave it to her for their anniversary. They got to know each other around this time last year.

The thought that Vin just went ahead and celebrated their anniversary makes me even more nauseous than Romy's driving.

I tear my eyes away from the ankle chain and watch as Romy overtakes a truck and moves across two lanes in one go.

"So I'm not allowed to know anything about where we're going?" I try again. Nova knows I hate surprises, doesn't she?

"You don't need to know anything," says Nova. "Reid Hunter thought it was a perfect idea, and that's exactly what it is."

"Reid Hunter?" I echo.

"I had those student adviser sessions with him at the end of March, remember? I told him what I was planning, and he thought it made perfect sense to go somewhere nice and peaceful before exams." Nova is still drumming on her legs. "Anyway, I let your mom and dad know exactly where we're going, and Romy has the location."

The location, as if we're off to dig up treasure somewhere . . .

"Well, I know where we're going," says Vin. "But I promised to keep my mouth shut."

"That's right." Nova flaps the mirror down and gives him a stern look. "Or you'll have me to deal with."

"I need something to drink," Romy says.

When she parks at the gas station, Nova is the first to jump out of the car.

A few minutes ago, to my surprise, we crossed the border and drove into West Virginia. Nova didn't even say we were going to leave the state.

"Anyone else want something?"

Vin squeezes out from under Nova's suitcase. He stands in front of the car and does a big stretch. I can see the edge of his boxer shorts.

"Get me a soda," he says.

"How about you?" Nova looks at me.

"No, thanks." I quickly take my phone out of my bag and slip it into my back pocket. How am I going to turn this thing on without anyone seeing?

Nova and Romy walk off together, leaving me behind with Vin. My heart rate shoots up, as if I have to do an important audition.

Vin takes out a water bottle and fills a bowl for Spot.

Spot hesitates for a moment. He's always a bit timid when Vin is around, like he doesn't quite know what to do. Maybe that's my fault. . . .

"Go on, boy," says Vin. "I brought it especially for you."

"Sweet."

Vin looks at me from behind his long bangs. "Hey, I can be pretty sweet sometimes."

Here we go. Nova's only been gone two seconds.

"Yeah, I know." Any minute now he's going to start talking about my message. I don't want him to do that, not with Nova around.

"Do you know . . . ," I quickly begin. "Do you know how much longer we have to drive?"

"Well, it's seriously in the middle of nowhere," says Vin. "But I'm not going to tell you any more than that, because she'll kill me."

There's an awkward silence. Nova really would kill us if she knew what we were hiding from her. . . .

We watch Spot emptying the bowl. Vin pours in some more water.

"Lotus?" Vin says, breaking the silence. "When we get there, I really need to talk to you."

See, I knew he couldn't just leave it alone.

"No, we can't," I say quietly. "Nova hears and sees everything."

"Not everything," Vin says firmly.

I head into the restroom at the rear of the gas station. I carefully close the door behind me. I sit down, turn on my phone, and count the seconds until it starts up.

First there's a message from my provider: Welcome to West Virginia!

But then my phone buzzes again, and the unknown number appears.

> Don't think you'll be rid of me when you get to that farmhouse.

I stare at the words on my screen. *That farmhouse,* it says. How can Unknown know about that? None of us has said anything about where we're going. Nova is way too scared that half the school will want to come party. And we really do need to concentrate on exams.

I swing open the door of my stall. In the mirror above the sink, I see my face, white as a sheet.

I call the number again, but still no one answers.

Who is doing this? And above all: Why? Is it someone I know? Someone who wants to scare me?

Then suddenly the image from last night flashes into my mind. That shadow by the bridge in the woods.

Was that who sent me the first message not long after?

I try to remember what the figure looked like, but they were too far away. Fifty yards, maybe more. And they were wearing dark, shapeless clothing. I couldn't even tell for sure if it was a man or a woman!

Don't think you'll be rid of me when you get to that farmhouse.

I think about Spot, who growled when he saw that person. Would he growl again if they started sneaking around outside the farmhouse?

Unless they're already *inside* the farmhouse?

I picture Nova, with her new gold ankle chain, her bare feet up on the dash, super enthusiastic about being away from home and undisturbed for a whole week.

What if Nova didn't book the farmhouse to study in, but to get Vin and me alone? Because she *knows*?

"Shit . . . ," I whisper at the mirror. "Vin . . ."

Then the toilet flushes. Romy comes out of the stall next to mine and casually tucks her phone into her bra.

"What's up with Vin?" she asks, turning on the faucet.

As I stare at the phone, which is still sticking out of her bra, I feel my cheeks burning. Could Romy have sent those messages? She's crazy enough—and she'd do anything for her sister. She and Nova are super close. I always used to be jealous of them, because Warner and I don't have that kind of bond at all.

"Nothing," I say quickly.

"I thought you guys were doing a complete lockdown," Romy says, pointing at my phone, which I'm still holding.

My cheeks blaze even hotter.

"I . . . I brought it along by accident."

Romy raises one eyebrow. "Better stash it somewhere quickly. If my sister finds out you're breaking the rules, she'll end you."

SUMMER

One girl in the class rolled her eyes when I introduced myself.

She was sitting right at the front, looking at me like I'd never be capable of saying something that interested her.

In my head, I named her Bittersweet.

Her voice was as sweet as honey, but she seemed so bitter.

This was someone I needed to stay far away from.

I was way too early today, but I always like to be the first to arrive.

I noticed I was humming to myself as I looked for my place.

The toffee melted slowly on my tongue.

Except for Bittersweet, no one did anything unpleasant yesterday.

This school is a new start—everything has to go well this time.

But then I saw the whiteboard.

There was a drawing on it: a stick figure with a belly so big that her blouse had burst open.

And beneath it was my name, in curly letters.

The artist had underlined the name, as if I might miss the point otherwise.

In a trance, I erased the drawing.

Day 2.

And it had already started again.

A few more hours and it'll begin.

LOTUS

Every mile we drive, it feels as if the noose around my neck is getting tighter.

I have to get out of this car. I have to go home. But instead, we're driving deeper and deeper into West Virginia. Nova's singing along to a song on the radio. Whenever she gets a word wrong, she looks back and smiles.

Her radiant eyes seem so honest.

Is she really that good at acting?

Romy finally takes an exit. I can't wait to get out of the car. I need fresh air. I need to think.

We slow down and drive through a small town with a fountain and a minimart. Could this be the middle of nowhere Vin was talking about?

But then we leave the town and drive into the forest. All I can see are trees, trees, and more trees. The sun barely penetrates the dense canopy, and the trees are so huge that I feel like a toy doll.

Under normal circumstances, I would love this place, far away from all the hustle and bustle, but now it feels like we're driving toward an abyss.

The hard road surface turns into a sandy track. Romy tries to steer around the bumps and potholes.

"There it is!" Nova takes her feet off the dash and slips them into her shoes.

On a small hill, a big farmhouse with a red-tiled roof looms up out of the trees. It has a big balcony that wraps all around the house.

Romy parks the car in front of the closed garage door and pulls the hand brake.

Spot is the first to jump out of the car. I go after him and grab his leash off the ground. Mom made it very clear: Spot isn't allowed off the leash, because he's sure to follow any interesting scents, and this place must be full of tasty wild animals.

"Wow . . ." Vin swings Nova's suitcase out of the car. "This is even more beautiful than in the photos."

"Nice, huh?" Nova wraps her arms around him and presses a kiss to his lips. I used to be fine with them doing that stuff when I was around, but now I can't bear to look.

"What do you think?" Nova asks me.

"Amazing," I say. "Really beautiful."

"Just wait until you see inside." Nova picks up her

suitcase and walks to the front door, which is next to the garage. She fishes a key from her pocket and turns it in the lock.

As Nova and Vin head inside, I stand by the car with Spot. I look at the rows of trees surrounding the farmhouse. Is Unknown bluffing, or are they somewhere in the forest right now, watching me? This is the perfect place to keep an eye on someone.

"Sorry you came along?"

I turn to look. It's Romy.

"No," I say quickly. "Why would I be sorry?"

"Hanging out with a couple of lovebirds? That doesn't sound like much fun to me. Third wheel and all that."

"I'm used to it," I say as calmly as I can.

"Yeah, and they're not as wild about each other as they used to be, right?" Romy says, looking straight at me. Her green eyes are like a self-scanner at the supermarket.

"W-what do you mean?"

"Well, they've been together for a year now. That first feeling of being in love fades and you start looking around again. But if Vin hurts Nova, I'm going to kill him."

I don't know where to look. What's Romy up to?

"Keep an eye on my sister while you're here, okay?"

I nod quickly. "Of course."

"Her food too?" Romy locks and unlocks the car with the fob. The noise is making me anxious. "You know what I mean, right?"

"Yeah." I know very well what Romy means. Nova sometimes eats so little that I don't know how she manages to function. If she has her way over the next week, she'll barely eat anything.

Romy locks the car for the last time. "I'm counting on you."

There are several doors leading off the main hallway. There's no sign of Vin and Nova, but I don't want to be alone with Romy for another second.

Choosing a door at random, I find myself in a large living room with a breakfast nook, an open fireplace, and two cozy red corduroy couches. The heads of two boars and a big bear look down at me from the walls, giving me a glassy stare. The bear's head is at a bit of an angle, so it really seems to be looking at me. Spot sometimes does that when he's waiting for something to happen.

I shiver. Why do people think hanging dead animals' heads on the wall lends atmosphere to a room? It feels like they could come back to life at any moment.

Spot barks at the bear, but then jumps onto one of the couches and curls up contentedly in the corner. At home, he's not allowed on the couch, but I let him up on the couch here.

On the dining table, there's a welcome package of tea

and chocolates. *Enjoy your stay,* it says on the card. I open it up and put a chocolate in my mouth.

When I look around, I see that Nova wasn't exaggerating. There's nothing here—no Wi-Fi, no TV.

On a small table in the corner, there's just an old-fashioned yellow telephone with a curly cord. I walk over to it and lift the receiver. The dial tone in my ear sounds strangely reassuring.

"Lotus, we're up here!"

When I look up, I see Nova and Vin leaning over the railing of the balcony that overlooks the living room.

"How did you get up there?"

"Seek and you shall find," Nova says, pulling Vin away.

I open another door and find the bathroom, the walls covered with old-fashioned green tiles.

The next door leads to a bedroom with two made-up beds. Behind the last door, I finally find the stairs, which creak even worse than the old wooden floors.

On the landing, I find three more bedrooms. How many people can sleep here? I hope Nova doesn't suggest that Romy stay the night. I can't stand the thought of being stuck with her any longer.

Could it be Romy who sent those messages? It's possible. The way she just looked at me when she said that people stop being so wild about each other after a year . . .

I open some more doors. All the bedrooms on this

floor have a view out over the trees. So much more beautiful than the gray mass of new houses that I look out at when I'm home.

Then I find the most beautiful room of all. It has a double bed and French doors that open onto the roof terrace. I open them and step outside. It hits me just how quiet it is here. The only sound is coming from the leaves, rustling softly in the wind.

I walk up to the balcony's railing and rest my hands on the wood, which is still a little warm from the sun.

For a moment, it's as if I can feel his arms wrapped around me. What would it be like if we were here as a couple?

We'd spend night after night kissing and talking.

No, don't think about that.

I've put a stop to it. It's over.

For good.

The buzz in my pocket startles me. I used to love that sound, because I knew it had to be him, but now it feels more like a fire alarm.

Beautiful here, isn't it?

I gasp, as if stung by a wasp.

Did Romy send the message? From up here, I can see her standing by the car, looking bored as she scrolls through her phone.

Would she really risk sending it when she's standing in plain sight?

Without hesitating, I call the number. If it's Romy, she should react.

I'm staring so hard at her that my eyes start to water, but nothing happens. Romy doesn't look up or around. She stands there, looking just as bored as ever.

So who is the message from?

I stare at the words, as if they were handwritten and I might be able to figure something out from the hand-writing.

"Admiring the pool?"

I spin around to see Vin standing there, with his hands in his pockets. Quickly, I hide my phone behind my back.

"The pool?" I echo.

"There."

I look to the right of the farmhouse and see a rectangular swimming pool down there, full of ice-blue water.

"It's not too bad here, eh? Maybe we can go for a dip when we're not studying." Vin looks at me. "Feeling a bit better?"

"What . . . what do you mean?"

"Your car sickness."

I've never felt so nauseous, but it has nothing to do with the car.

"Yeah. Yeah, it's fine."

Vin smiles, his brown eyes sparkling. "You coming downstairs? Nova and I have a surprise for you."

Nova and I.

How can he keep this up? Sometimes I feel like I'm going to burst from all the lies inside me.

"I'll be down in a minute," I say. "You go ahead."

After Vin disappears into the master bedroom, I take my phone from behind my back.

Beautiful here, isn't it?

I want to delete the words, but instead I just keep staring at them. If it's not Romy or Nova, the possibilities are endless.

Unknown could be anyone, and I don't think they have any intention of making themselves known.

I squeeze my phone. It's not fair. I know I've made some bad choices, but it's not just my fault. We did this together, and as far as I know, no one's bothering him.

I wonder if I should call the number again, but I'm certain no one will answer, so instead I begin to type. My thumbs flash over the letters, as if, all this time, I've known what I wanted to say. Without thinking about it, I send the message.

Leave me alone, asshole.

SUMMER

This afternoon, I was about to head home, but my bike was acting weird.

And then I realized what the problem was: my back tire was flat.

I saw Bittersweet watching me from a distance.

She smiled—and it looked like a challenge.

Pushing the bike, I walked away.

The repair guy told me it wasn't just a normal puncture. Someone had taken a knife to it.

"They really had it in for this tire, miss," he said, looking at me sympathetically. "You been making enemies?"

LOTUS

Romy is about to leave when Nova stops her.

"Are you sure you want to go home? We have plenty of beds here."

See, there it is. What if Romy accepts the offer? I'll be stuck with her for days.

But Romy smiles and shakes her head. "You guys need to study, remember? I'd only distract you."

"Yeah, I know." Nova glances at Vin and me.

I know Nova hates saying goodbye. I think that's one of the reasons why she chose to go to the same high school as me, even though it's a much longer bike ride for her.

Romy closes the car door, but then rolls down the window. "Want me to do some grocery shopping for you in town?"

Nova shakes her head. "Lotus and I will go on the

bikes. We need a bit of exercise today. My butt's just about numb from the journey here."

"Okay." Romy blows a kiss as she drives away. After a few yards, she hits the gas and the car disappears in a big cloud of dust.

"Do you want that one?" Nova points at the mountain bike partially covered by a sheet in the corner of the garage. The two of us are going into town. Vin is staying behind to unpack the rest of the things and keep an eye on Spot.

I look around. I'm surprised to see how much stuff is in here: from a lawn mower to multiple boxes of tools. When I pull the mountain bike out from under an old sheet of canvas, I spot it right away.

"The tire's flat."

"Then pump it up." Nova nods to a bicycle pump in the corner.

I'm about to bend down to unscrew the cap when I see a hole in the rubber. Looks like someone rode over a big piece of glass.

"That's not going to work. The tire's punctured. Can I go on the back of your bike?"

"As soon as we get to paved road," Nova says, riding her bike out of the garage. "Let's hope the store's still open when we finally get there."

"Maybe we should have accepted Romy's offer," I say as Nova struggles to push the bike through the loose sand.

"Hey, I can cope without Romy's help," Nova snaps.

"I didn't say you couldn't, did I?"

"Well, that's what Vin thinks. He thinks I'm way too clingy with Romy."

I kind of understand what Vin means.

"I just don't like being alone," says Nova. "There's nothing wrong with that, is there?"

I shake my head. "Maybe you should tell him why."

Nova raises her eyebrows. "No way. And you're not going to tell him either."

"My lips are sealed," I say quickly.

I look at the rows of trees beside the track. Again, I feel like someone's watching me.

My phone is back at the farmhouse. Did my angry message help? Maybe Unknown will just leave me alone from now on and I'll never find out who they are.

"What was your surprise, by the way?" I ask.

"Oh, that." Nova smiles. "We want to give you the big bedroom."

"Why?" I ask, shocked. It's the only room with a double bed, so I assumed Vin and Nova would take it.

"Because you deserve it." Nova looks at me. "Don't you?"

She gives me the same once-over that Romy did earlier.

"Yes," I say quickly. "I think I do."

Nova sighs. "So just enjoy it. Have you seen that view?"

"It's amazing," I say. "The most beautiful bedroom in the house."

Nova holds out her leg. "What do you think of my new ankle chain, by the way?"

I see the gold anklet sticking up above the edge of her shoe.

"I noticed it in the car. Was it a gift?"

"Got it from Vin, for our anniversary."

See, their anniversary. A stab of jealousy shoots through me. I'll never be able to celebrate something like that with him. And now that it's all over for good, it's never going to happen.

I feel tears in my eyes and quickly blink them away. There's no point thinking about that. Putting an end to it was the best choice I could have made.

"I was actually surprised that Vin remembered," Nova continues. "Lately he's been so . . . distant."

The soft dirt suddenly feels like quicksand. It was inevitable that Nova would start to notice the cracks in her relationship with Vin, but now that the time has come, I wish we were somewhere other than miles away from home.

"Maybe he's stressed out because of exams?" I suggest.

"But Vin's usually super relaxed, isn't he?"

We're finally at the paved road, and I gratefully jump onto the back of Nova's bike. Anything is better than having to look at her while she talks about Vin.

Nova speeds up and we shoot past the rows of trees. "So, you have no idea why he's acting strange?"

"Me?" I can feel my hands sweating, almost sliding off the metal of the bike. "How should I know?"

"Well, maybe he said something to you?"

"No."

"Then maybe you could talk to him for me? You know, just ask him if something's bothering him, or something."

Not a chance. Nova feels my hesitation and looks back over her shoulder at me. The bike swerves dangerously.

"It's driving me crazy, Lotus. What if he thinks I'm fat?"

"Fat?" I look in horror at the slim waist in front of me. The past couple of years, Nova has lost so much weight that I hardly recognize her in our old class photos.

Keep an eye on my sister. I'm counting on you.

"You're not seriously worried about that, are you?" I manage to say. "That's the dumbest thing I've ever heard."

"Of course not." Nova quickly brushes it off. "And anyway, if he does think that, he can totally drop dead."

We leave the store with two big bags full of groceries. We got there just in time, right before the store closed.

"Back to the farmhouse," says Nova. "Before it gets dark."

"How about I ride back?" I suggest.

"Yeah, thanks." Nova hangs the two heavy bags on the handlebars. "Then I'll cook."

I know exactly why she's suggesting that. Last Christmas, she let it slip. She said that she made the Christmas dinner at home because then she knew exactly which ingredients were in the food—that is, how many calories. That gives her one hundred percent control: no creamy sauces, nothing too fattening.

Romy was right. We have to keep an eye on her.

"You can cook tonight," I say. "But if it's inedible, I'm taking over tomorrow."

Nova nods. "Deal. Now get cycling, before it's dark!"

I feel it as soon as I climb onto the bike.

A wave of panic washes over me as I look at the back tire, which is completely flat. "Another puncture."

I just about crush the phone in my hand.
    asshole
    The word echoes inside my head.
    How dare she.

LOTUS

"What the hell took you so long?"

When we finally arrive, Vin is waiting at the door. His face is white as a sheet.

"I thought something had happened to you!"

"Sorry." Nova lifts one of the heavy grocery bags off the handlebars.

"Our back tire had a puncture, and we obviously had no way to contact you without our phones."

Vin sighs. "Yeah, great plan, this lockdown."

"You said it was a really good idea," Nova reminds him.

"Anything could have happened!"

"Hey, chill." Nova sighs.

I know what Vin means, but we're here now, aren't we? He never usually gets upset like this. He must have been really worried about us.

"The good news is, we got the groceries," I say, trying to make peace.

"Exactly." Nova looks at me. "Will you put the bike away, Lotus?"

"Sure."

Nova disappears inside with the grocery bags, and I push the bike into the garage. The bulb on the ceiling sways when I pull the cord. The garage fills with yellow light, and the stuff in the corners looks like people watching me from the shadows.

I bend over the bike and study the now-flat tire. Did we ride over something on the way into town?

"You okay?"

Vin is standing in the doorway, under the light, his shadow stretching across the wall.

"Yeah, I'm fine," I say quickly. "I just want to fix this tire."

"Do you know how?"

"No need to sound so surprised. My dad taught me and Warner. He thought it would come in handy for emergencies."

"Well, this is an emergency." Vin brushes a strand of hair out of his face. "I was terrified when you guys didn't come back."

"Sorry."

"It's okay." Vin walks over to me.

"I don't get how this tire could suddenly go flat." I turn

the bike upside down so I can take a closer look at the damage.

"You want a flashlight?" Vin takes a ring of keys out of his pocket, with a mini flashlight attached.

"Wow. That's a lot of keys," I say as I click the flashlight on. There must be, like, seven keys here.

"Divorced parents," Vin reminds me. "That's what you get. Two of everything."

"I'd hate that," I admit. "Switching houses every weekend. That must suck."

"I only sleep at my mom's once a month. She doesn't have much room, so that's okay for now. Besides, I get whatever I want at my dad's." Vin smiles. "The divorce was his fault, you know. He went off with another woman. So now he's overcompensating. I know it's wrong, but sometimes I do take advantage of it."

I know exactly what he means. Vin's dad is always really friendly, but he tries so hard that it almost becomes awkward.

"I needed a new bag for this trip, so I said a big backpack would come in handy for when I had to travel between him and Mom *yet again.* . . ."

I burst out laughing. "You have him wrapped around your little finger!"

"I know." Vin puts his hands in the air. "Guilty as charged."

I shine Vin's flashlight on the tire. It looks like a wild animal ripped into the rubber. There's a huge hole in it.

I also take a look at the other bike. It takes a while, but I eventually find the culprit. It's not a big slash, but clearly more than a hole from a simple pushpin or nail.

Is it a coincidence or did someone intentionally destroy our tires? Someone who wanted us to have no transportation.

Don't think you'll be rid of me when you get to that farmhouse.

Is this what Unknown meant? Was it them who punctured our tires? How did they do it?

A thousand thoughts are racing through my mind.

"So?" asks Vin. "Can you fix the tires?"

"Yep," I say quickly. "But I'll do it later. It's too dark now."

"And?" Nova asks, looking hopefully at me over her dinner plate. There are three lit candles between us. The animal heads on the walls watch in silence. The bear is still at a bit of an angle. Its eyes are like two black marbles, dull and dead.

"Delicious," I admit. It hasn't escaped my notice that Nova's plate is a lot less full than Vin's and mine. She's also given herself mainly salad and much less of the pasta.

"Phew," says Nova. "Okay, then you and Vin can wash the dishes."

Me and Vin. I can already picture us, shoulder to shoulder, at the counter. I bet he'll try to speak to me again.

"Cool." Vin scoops up the last of the pasta from his plate. "But how about going for a quick dip first?"

"Now?" Nova's eyes are twinkling. In one movement, she pulls her blouse over her head. Before I can react, she's running in her bra toward the doors.

Vin goes after her, pulling off his T-shirt as he goes. Spot is a close third. I watch them running across the terrace and a few seconds later I hear two splashes.

I push back my chair and follow them outside. Spot is wagging his tail by the side of the pool.

The lights around the pool are powered by solar energy and give off a warm, flickering glow. Above the pool, a cloud of steam evaporates into the air.

"Come on in!" Nova waves her bra and throws it at me. "Come on!"

To my surprise, Vin's boxer shorts are lying on the edge of the pool too, right next to Nova's discarded blouse. I stare at them for a moment.

Skinny-dipping with Nova? Okay. But with Vin there? So awkward . . .

"Oh, come on!" Nova splashes some water at me. I know she'll keep insisting until I say yes.

"Okay, okay."

Slowly, I get undressed and put my clothes in a folded pile on one of the loungers. It's cold—I hope the water's better. Standing outside in my underwear, I suddenly feel much more vulnerable. When I take off my bra, I immediately regret it, but I keep going. In my panties, I walk to the ladder and lower myself into the water, which is surprisingly warm.

"That's cheating," says Nova, pointing at my panties.

"Yep, then so be it." No way am I getting completely naked.

"Go on," urges Nova. "All of us should be naked. It's part of the inauguration for Nerd Central. Starting tomorrow, we'll be serious, but not tonight. Tomorrow morning, I'll make breakfast in bed for you, with those pancakes you like so much. I promise. It's just the three of us. No one else is going to see you."

I think about Unknown. Who says they're not somewhere out there, watching from the sidelines?

But then I remember my phone, which I checked again just before dinner. There's still no answer. Unknown really does seem to have been scared off by my angry message.

I look again at the dense bushes around the swimming pool. I can't seriously imagine anyone hiding in there. That flat tire was just stupid bad luck.

"Fine." With a sigh, I take off my panties, and before I can react, Nova snatches them from my hand. They fly through the air and land with a splat somewhere on the side of the pool.

"What are you doing?!"

"Then you can't change your mind." Nova floats on her back. "Admit it. This is amazing, isn't it?"

I don't want to say that she's right, but fair's fair: This is indeed amazing. This is what freedom feels like. My body relaxes, and I surrender to the water.

"Before long we'll have passed our exams," Vin says after a few minutes. "Then we'll be done with school."

"Hmm . . . ," I hum. "And then I'll be studying veterinary medicine."

"You still want to do that?" Vin asks. "It's a tough choice."

"So what?" says Nova. "Lotus and I want to get even smarter than we already are."

Nova and I have always planned on going to the same school and becoming vets together, but is that really what she wants? Nova is crazy about Spot, but I really don't see her becoming a vet.

"Well, count me out," says Vin.

Nova sighs. "You're just running away."

I look at her. "What do you mean?"

"Vin's going to *travel*." Nova says it like Vin's planning to commit a murder.

"Where to?" I ask curiously.

Nova stands up in the water. "What difference does that make? It's just a really dumb plan."

"Don't start again." Vin makes a face. "It's *my* plan. You don't have to come."

"No, exactly."

Suddenly I understand what the problem is. It's not bad that Vin's going traveling; it's bad that Nova is staying behind, alone. Is that why she's following me to college?

"I'll come back," says Vin.

"After *six* months?" Nova splutters. "Don't bother."

"Ten months," Vin corrects her. "And why are you being so hostile? We've talked about this, haven't we? I'll come back to visit, and we can keep in touch by—"

Spot barks. The noise, which booms across the water, makes all three of us jump. Spot is standing in front of one of the bushes by the pool and backing away a little.

It looks familiar. It's what he did in the woods too.

I swim to the side and pull myself out of the water. Is someone there after all? I completely forget that I'm naked. My legs feel like elastic as I walk over to Spot, who's still barking.

Vin hoists himself onto the side too. "I bet he can smell wild animals."

Spot's barking like mad now. What if Unknown really is watching us from the bushes? I see those shapeless black clothes again. The thought paralyzes me.

"Hello?" I call. I peer into the dark bushes, but I can't see anything. I pick up a flashlight from the ground beside me, but then Spot stops barking.

"You see, must have been a deer." When I turn around, Vin has put his boxers back on. "Nothing to worry about."

Quickly, I walk to my pile of clothes. Where are my panties? Nova threw them onto the side, didn't she?

I can't find them anywhere, so I just pull my pants on. It's not easy—the fabric keeps sticking to my wet legs.

"We're getting out?" Nova calls from the pool.

"Yes." No way I'm going skinny-dipping with Unknown nearby.

Nova climbs onto the side too. Now that I'm seeing her without clothes, I can really see how much weight she's lost. When she pulls her blouse over her head, I can count her ribs.

"Okay, then," she sighs. "Spoilsports."

"Come on." I pat the comforter again, but Spot stays on the floor, looking at me. At home, he always sleeps downstairs in his crate, but I want to keep him with me tonight, just to be on the safe side.

It's late, and I've been worried all night about Vin wanting to talk again. But Nova didn't leave us on our own for a moment, not even while we were washing the dishes, so it didn't happen.

Luckily, Spot peed in the flower bed beside the pool, because I don't even want to think about having to let him out in the dark.

"Here, boy," I say. When I pat my bed for the third time, Spot jumps up onto the mattress and snuggles beside me.

I switch off the lamp on the bedside table and my eyes slowly adjust to the dark. The phone under my pillow is silent. Unknown hasn't been in touch again.

Have I gotten rid of them?

But who or what was Spot barking at? Could it have been a deer or some other animal?

In the room next to mine, Nova and Vin are laughing. It sounds like they're having fun, seems they've completely forgotten the argument they had in the pool.

The laughter turns into silence. They're kissing now, for sure.

I roll onto my side. Spot's already asleep and snoring a bit. His breath stinks, but his warm body feels safe.

The curtains gently sway in front of the open window. The doors to the balcony are firmly shut—I checked three times. Absolutely nothing can get to me here.

Spot's regular breathing has a hypnotic effect, and I feel my own eyes begin to close.

I don't know what wakes me, but when I open my eyes, the curtains are flapping wildly in the breeze. I hear the bedroom door creaking, followed by cautious footsteps.

There's someone in my room!

I hold my breath and lie still under the covers. My whole body is on the alert, ready to lash out.

Why isn't Spot doing anything?

I have to call for help. Nova and Vin are so close, but it feels like my throat is locked and I've lost the key.

The footsteps come closer, then seem to hesitate for a moment.

I feel Spot move. Is he finally waking up? Any minute now, he's going to bark, like he did by the pool.

But then I feel a hand over my mouth. It happens so quickly that I can't react. My scream is muffled by a sweaty palm.

"Shhh, quiet!" The voice by my ear makes all the tension flow out of my body. Vin?

I hold my breath and feel his hand slide from my mouth.

"What are you doing?" I hiss at him. "You nearly gave me a heart attack, you idiot!"

"Keep your voice down." Vin flicks on the lamp beside me. His hair is all over the place. He's looking anxiously at the half-open bedroom door.

"I know it's the middle of the night, but I need to talk to you. Nova's asleep."

Spot jumps off the bed and goes to lie in a corner of the room. He keeps a close eye on Vin.

"Listen." Vin looks at me seriously. "I don't want you to say anything to Nova."

Is that all he can think about? About Nova? I feel fury bubbling up inside me. Does he have any idea how hard this is for me?

"Sometimes it's better to keep silent."

He really means it. Vin wants to pretend nothing happened.

"Do it for me. For us. If you tell the truth, that's the end of the three of us." Vin is staring at me, his dark eyes pleading. "Then Nova won't want anything more to do with me, and she won't want anything to do with you either. You know how mad she can get."

I know exactly what he means. There have been plenty of times when we've shared worried looks as Nova suddenly exploded again.

"She already knows something is going on," I say. "She thinks you've been acting weird lately. She thinks you think she's fat."

"*Fat?!*" Vin bursts out laughing. "When I touch her, all I can feel is bones."

"Yes, I know that. But she's not exactly thinking clearly."

I have to keep my mouth shut. Nova will kill me if she finds out I've been talking to Vin about this.

"I'll try harder."

What exactly does he mean by that? Kiss her more persuasively?

Vin puts his hand on my arm. I look at his fingers, which feel warm and rough on my skin.

"Vin?" A sleepy voice from the landing. "Where are you?"

Vin pulls back his hand and jumps to his feet. "I'm here!"

"In Lotus's room?" A surprised Nova sticks her head

around the door. Spot immediately trots over to her. "What are you doing?"

"I . . . I was looking for the bathroom." Vin doesn't sound very convincing. "But I opened the wrong door."

"The bathroom is downstairs," says Nova, her gaze lingering on me.

"Back in a minute." Vin hurries downstairs. Nova stands there in the doorway.

"Is that true?" she asks. "Was Vin really looking for the bathroom?"

"Yes." I feel my cheeks burning. I just hope the lamplight isn't bright enough for her to see that. "Of course."

"I thought I heard you talking."

"He . . . he's worried about you," I quickly say. "And so am I."

Nova makes a face. "Why?"

"That dinner." I take a deep breath. "You're not eating enough."

Nova smiles. "Then there's more for you two, isn't there?"

I ignore her lame attempt at a joke. "You've lost a lot of weight."

I look at the baggy nightshirt that Nova's wearing. If she weren't so toned, her legs would look like a couple of matchsticks.

"I just watch what I eat." Nova releases a deep sigh. "That's all."

There's no point talking to her. She'll only deny it.

"Find something else to worry about." Nova looks me in the eye. "Okay?"

I feel the lump of my phone under the pillow. Downstairs, the toilet flushes, followed by Vin's footsteps on the stairs.

"Sleep tight." Nova closes the door behind her.

When I wake up for the second time, I have a headache.

Spot is down on the floor, slowly pulling the comforter off my bare legs.

I'm not ready to wake up. I was still in the middle of a dream.

"What are you doing?" I mumble, taking my phone out from under the pillow. It's only half past six! At home, I always prefer to take Spot for his evening walk—and there's a reason for that. I hate getting up early, but Spot doesn't give up and starts whimpering quietly. He's just like Nova: whenever he wants something, he keeps insisting.

"Okay, okay. We're going." With a sigh, I swing my legs over the edge of the bed. My head is thumping as if I've been partying half the night.

I'm about to head for the door when I suddenly spot something hanging over the chair. It takes a second, but then the realization hits me like a thunderbolt.

I lean forward and snatch my panties from the armrest.

They're still a bit damp from the pool, but otherwise it's as if they've been hanging here all this time.

Spot spins in circles around my legs, but I stand there with the panties in my hand.

I couldn't find them after Nova threw them aside last night. So how can they be here now?

Did Vin put them there when he came to talk last night? I know for certain they weren't there last night when I went to sleep. . . .

My phone buzzes, as if it's come to rescue me with the answer.

> Don't get so mad, okay? Next time
> I'll steal more than just your panties.

It was a huge risk, but I had to do it.
   She shouldn't have sent that message.
   It's a good thing that the dog liked my treats.

SUMMER

I felt the ball of paper fly into the back of my head.

It was just paper, but it hit me like a brick.

When I turned around, Bittersweet was smiling at me.

"Something wrong?"

I went on writing, but my hand was shaking so much that the letters were a mess.

"Go on," I heard Bittersweet egging someone else on.

The next one came from a different direction.

The balls of paper kept coming, all lesson long.

By the time the bell rang, it looked like it had been snowing in the classroom.

During the break, Reid Hunter came and sat beside me in the sunshine.

"How's it going so far?"

"Good," I said, but I could feel the lump in my throat moving at the same time.

"Great."

The three of them were walking past.

Bittersweet glanced at me, but when she saw I wasn't alone, she kept going.

"That ugly face makes me feel so nauseous," I heard Bittersweet say. "She thinks she's some kind of big deal."

Was she talking about me?

But I didn't think I was a big deal. No way!

"The weather's going to be fabulous this weekend." Reid Hunter hadn't even noticed the conversation I was trying to listen in on. "Planning anything fun?"

I shrugged. "Working in the garden with my dad, I think."

"You have a garden?"

"Yeah."

Reid Hunter grinned. "So do I. We have a large plot of land. I can spend hours in nature."

I nodded. "Yeah, I know that feeling."

He smiled. "Plant nerds—that's what we are."

We.

It sounded good.

"My girlfriend doesn't get it. But then, she's an English teacher." Reid raised his hand, the gold wedding ring sparkling in the sunlight. "Correction: *wife*. We've been married a month."

"Congratulations."

I focused on Bittersweet again, who was standing nearby.

When our gazes met, she slowly drew her index finger across her throat.

LOTUS

Unknown isn't bluffing. My last remnant of doubt dissolves like a sugar cube in tea.

Unknown was here, in my room. What did they do? Just hang up my panties, or stand there watching me sleep? A wave of panic washes over me.

"Stupid dog," I say to Spot. "Why didn't you bark?"

"You're not having another conversation with the dog, are you?" Nova is standing in the doorway behind me with a tray in her hands. Quickly, I stuff my phone into the waistband of my pajamas.

"What's wrong? You look like you've seen a ghost."

In my mind, I picture Unknown, here in this room. Standing beside me, in those scary, black clothes.

Why didn't I wake up?

And why didn't Nova and Vin notice anything?

How did Unknown get into the farmhouse? I checked the doors of the roof terrace three times! And I'm absolutely certain that everything was locked downstairs.

Spot jumps on Nova, who quickly puts down the tray on my bedside table and gives him a tickle behind the ears.

"Calm down." Nova laughs. "Did you wake Lotus up? Is that why she's so grumpy?"

Spot wags his tail furiously. With a thud, the realization hits me. Spot didn't bark last night. So there's only one possibility: Unknown is someone I know.

"Did you bring back my panties last night?" My throat feels as dry as sandpaper. What if my first theory turns out to be right? What if Nova is behind these dumb stunts?

Nova looks at me blankly. "What are you talking about?"

"Just answer the question!"

"Hey, don't go getting all worked up!" Nova gently pushes Spot away. "I bring you breakfast in bed and this is what I get?"

"What's going on?" Vin sticks his head around the door. He still has bedhead.

Was it him? Did he come back after our conversation? *I don't want you to say anything to Nova.*

Is this his way of trying to get me to keep quiet? By scaring me to death? I look at how tall Vin is. It could easily have been him in the woods.

"Lotus thinks I stole her underwear," Nova says to Vin.

"I want to know how my panties got here." I point outside. "Last night at the pool, I couldn't find them anywhere and now they're suddenly hanging over the chair!"

Nova frowns. "So you think one of us snuck them back in here last night?"

Vin smiles. "Sorry, Lotus, but that makes no sense."

Pulling Spot with me, I squeeze past Vin and onto the landing.

"What are you doing?" Nova shouts after me.

"Going out."

"What about breakfast? I used the tea from the welcome package, and I made pancakes and . . ."

I'm already downstairs, and I throw the front door open. In front of the farmhouse, I take a few deep breaths, but it doesn't really help. I want to scream and scream and scream until my voice goes hoarse.

What on earth is going on? What is Unknown up to? Are they trying to drive me crazy?

Well, they're doing a pretty good job of it. I feel like I've ended up in some kind of bad horror movie.

Spot suddenly tugs on the leash, dragging me away from the farmhouse. I have to run to keep up with him, and I almost trip over a fallen tree branch.

I have to keep all my attention on the ground so that I don't stumble as we go deeper into the forest.

"Easy, boy," I shout, but strangely the running helps. I always used to go running when I was angry, and this feels kind of the same. The fury in my body is starting to fade.

The trees aren't scary anymore. There's something mysterious about the morning mist.

When Spot has had enough of running, I stand there panting.

"I need to be careful, Spot," I say quietly. "Nova and Vin both deny having anything to do with it, so who is it? Romy?"

I think about Nova's sister, who went tearing away down the sandy track just yesterday. Maybe Romy didn't go back home at all.

Spot suddenly stops. His front paw goes into the air and he sniffs. I recognize that position—it means he's smelled something tasty.

"No, Spot." I look around. The sun is up, but I'm still cold. The mist that seemed so mysterious and beautiful a moment ago is suddenly suffocating. My fear is back. I should never have strayed so far from the farmhouse.

"Let's go back."

I turn around, but then I hear something rustling.

Spot pulls me with him with all the strength in his body.

The leash shoots out of my hand, and he runs off.

"No!" Stumbling, I go after him. If I lose him, my mom and dad will be so mad. Spot is like their third kid—Warner and I always make jokes about it.

It was hard enough to get them to agree to let him come with me, but Mom eventually decided it would be good for our safety. I have no idea why it felt safe to her, because Spot isn't a guard dog. He's a hunting dog! And now that he's got the scent of game, he's unstoppable.

I run after him as he disappears behind a row of trees. "Spot!"

I see him—his head is to the ground and he seems to be eating something. A bit of dead squirrel? Or a mouse?

But when I get closer, I recognize it. It's a bird, its feathers scattered over the ground.

"Come on," I say sternly. "We're going back."

Spot really doesn't want to come, but eventually I manage to pull him away from the bird.

Nova and Vin are going to have to explain how my panties ended up in my room. One of them must know more about it—or surely they must have heard someone?

Just as I spot the farmhouse's red roof tiles through the trees, I feel a buzz against my bare stomach.

It takes me a second to realize what it is, but then I remember: my cell. I fish the phone out from under the waistband of my pajama bottoms.

> Are you going to let your friends drink that delicious "herbal tea" from my welcome package all by themselves?

The words slowly take effect, like an anesthetic spreading through my body.

But it makes me more alert, instead of sleepy.

Herbal tea.

"No . . . Nova. Vin." I whisper their names—and then I start running.

SUMMER

"There you are."

Bittersweet came into the print room, where I was making photocopies.

"Let me be frank with you. I want you to fuck off."

The printer spat out three copies before I could even react.

"What do you mean?" I asked dumbly.

"I want you out of my school."

Bittersweet came closer.

Our noses were almost touching when she whispered: "Or I'll make sure you end up begging to leave."

"Sorry, I can't come in today. I really don't feel good."

"Oh, that's too bad." Reid Hunter was as friendly as ever. "Hope you feel better soon."

*   *   *

That Monday, I saw Bittersweet looking at me, but I just kept walking.

I wasn't going to let her win.

This time I was going to stay where I belonged.

After lunch, there was a new drawing on the board.

A massively fat stick figure in a coffin.

Underneath it said: *drop dead*.

I quickly erased it.

LOTUS

"Nova! Vin!" I run to the farmhouse, closely followed by Spot. The front door bangs against the wall as I storm in.

"Lotus?" Nova is sitting on the couch, a steaming cup of tea in her hands. "Is everything okay?"

"Don't!" I slap the mug out of her hands. As the hot tea pours over her fingers, she screams.

"What are you doing?" Nova jumps up furiously.

"Did you drink any?" My blood is fizzing like a bath bomb in water. "Did you take a sip?"

"You need to run cold water over that," I hear Vin saying as he leads Nova to the faucet. "Are you okay?"

"She's the one you should be asking!" Nova looks back at me, her eyes full of tears. "She is losing it."

"I asked you if you drank any of the tea!" I pull the lid

off the teapot and sniff the tea. It smells sweet, a bit like raspberry.

"Is there something wrong with the tea?" Vin gives me a searching look. "It tasted fine to me."

"Did you . . . ?" The room is spinning. What if Vin collapses? The nearest town is miles away and our bike tires are flat! I could call an ambulance, but how long until it gets here?

"Yeah, so what if I did?" Vin frowns. "What's wrong with it?"

"Vin, you need to make yourself vomit." I walk over to him. "Put your finger down your throat. Now!"

"Stop it!" Nova screams. "You're scaring me!"

I can feel tears burning in my eyes. They're both going to be really ill and it'll be my fault. I thought it was a welcome package from the owner. I didn't think twice about eating the stuff in it. Why would I?

"You don't get it. I . . ."

My phone buzzes again.

This time I don't just feel it. I *hear* it.

And I'm not the only one.

"Lotus?" Nova's eyes grow wide as I take out the antiquated device. "Did you bring a *phone*?"

I can't even respond. Stunned, I stare at the message that appears on my screen.

Only joking.

I release my breath, which apparently I'd been holding. Slowly, the words sink in. Unknown wanted this to happen. They wanted me to make a fool of myself by charging into the farmhouse like a wild bull.

And I'd completely fallen for it.

When I look up, I see Nova staring at my phone as if it's a hand grenade.

"What is that doing here?"

"I . . . I brought it with me. I had to."

Nova puts a damp dish towel over the burn on her hand, which looks red and painful. "Where did you get an old brick like that?"

Everything is about to come out. What will Nova say when she finds out? Maybe she'll call her sister to come get us. Or maybe she'll make me walk all the way home alone.

I've lost her, I know that for sure.

I look at her. I know every birthmark, every bit of hair that doesn't do what she wants it to. Her bright eyes, her chewed nails that she's always trying to grow out.

"This morning you were furious with me because of a pair of panties, then you throw boiling tea all over me, and now you go and pull out a phone even though we'd agreed we'd leave them at home! What kind of friend are you?"

"The worst." I whisper the words so quietly that only I can hear them.

"What did you say?"

"Someone's threatening me." When I say the words out loud, I realize how made up they sound. "I had to bring this phone, because the messages keep coming."

"What are you saying?" Nova's face is one big question mark.

"Here, read it for yourself." I open the conversation with Unknown and show it to Nova. From the very first message in the woods to the last words: *Only joking*.

"I . . . I thought it was actually true," I stammer. "That someone was trying to poison you. . . ."

Nova runs her eyes over the messages. Vin stands behind her and reads them with her.

It feels like I'm standing in front of my mom and dad, confessing that I stole money from them.

When Nova finally finishes reading, she looks up.

"What does this person have on you?"

My eyes flick to Vin, who almost invisibly shakes his head.

He wants to keep it all hidden, no matter the cost, but it's going to come out sometime. He knows that, doesn't he?

"I'm having . . . a secret relationship."

"A secret *what*?" Nova bursts out laughing. "Come on, Lotus. You sound like a sixty-year-old!"

"It's over," I add quickly. "You need to know that—it's done. I told him that, but . . ."

"What the hell are you talking about?" Nova's smile disappears when she hears my serious tone. "Who with?"

I take a deep breath, as if I need to pull the right words out of the air.

"With Reid Hunter."

FALL

There was a pizza-delivery guy at our front door.

"Your order?" he said. "That'll be fifty-five dollars and seventy cents, please."

I look in surprise at the stack of pizza boxes in his hands.

"But . . . I didn't order anything. I think you have the wrong address."

I was about to close the door, but the guy pointed at the nameplate.

"Schild?"

"Yes, that's my name."

"That's the name on the order," he said, handing me the boxes. "There's a note that it was urgent because you were so hungry."

"Aren't you going to school?"

The next Monday, my dad was standing at my bedroom door.

"I don't feel good."

"Again?"

Reid Hunter had sounded understanding again on the phone, but my dad was right: I couldn't stay home forever.

"Tomorrow," I said, pulling my comforter over my head. "I'll go in tomorrow."

"You're back!" Bittersweet was by the bike rack when I got there. "How were the pizzas?"

I ignored her and quickly locked my bike.

As I headed for the school building, Bittersweet put her arm around my shoulders.

"What's that I smell? You did take a shower this morning, didn't you?"

Inside my head, I answered her.

That she was the one who stank.

That she should shut her mouth.

But I didn't say anything.

* * *

"Did you know that pigs feel it when they're slaughtered?"

Bittersweet was talking so loudly that afternoon that I couldn't help but hear her.

"They're full of stress hormones. Because they *know*. That's why they stink so bad. It's fear. They know they're going to be slaughtered. They just don't know when."

LOTUS

"Reid Hunter? The *biology teacher,* Reid Hunter?"

The look on Vin's face is as incredulous as Nova's. He's looking at me like I just beamed down from another planet. Even after I just saved his ass. Confessing *our* secret would have been easier than spilling this one. But when I saw his pleading eyes, I couldn't do it.

"You mean our *married* teacher Reid Hunter?"

How many times is Nova going to repeat his name?

"To me, he's just Reid," I say.

"To you, he's just . . ." Nova looks at me, then Vin, and back again. "Goddammit. Sorry, but I can't listen to this."

"Nova . . ."

"No." Nova's eyes are spitting fire. "This is way too gross."

She throws open the door to the hallway. The whole

house shakes when she slams the door behind her, followed by the front door.

The silence in the kitchen is painful, but it becomes even more painful when Vin opens his mouth.

"Thank you."

"No," I say. "Don't start thanking me."

"I'm sorry, Lotus."

I feel all the energy flow out of me. This is just the beginning. When Nova comes back, I'm going to have to tell her everything.

How many times in the past year have I lied to her about extra tutoring?

Nova is pretty forgiving, as long as I don't lie to her.

"I need to be able to trust you, Lotus," she always says. "If I can't do that, you'll lose me."

I hear the sound of running water and Vin hands me a glass. "Here. She'll be back soon. Why don't you sit down?"

I look at the closed door.

"You'll just make it worse if you go after her now," Vin insists. "You know that, don't you?"

I know he's right, but still I have to make a real effort not to go storming out after her.

"Do you want to talk?" Vin sits down opposite me.

No, I think. *A thousand times no.*

But there isn't anyone else, and now that the first

sentence has crossed my lips, the rest wants to come out too.

"I have this phone especially for him, so that no one would find out. I'm not proud of it, if that's what you think."

"I don't think that at all." Vin leans across the table and puts his hand on mine. "Sounds like it'd be damn lonely."

I've never looked at it that way before, but ever since Reid Hunter became just Reid to me, that is how I feel. For the first time, I had a secret that was so big that I couldn't share it with anyone. Because who on earth could I tell? My mom and dad? They'd go crazy. Warner? My brother and I never talk about that kind of stuff. Vin? Maybe he was the only one who would understand.

But I didn't dare because of Nova. If I did something like that behind her back too . . .

"Nova will come around," says Vin. "If only out of curiosity. You know what she's like. I'd prepare for a cross-examination if I were you. She'll probably want to know exactly how you seduced him."

"He seduced me," I correct him.

"Really?" Vin's eyebrows shoot up, and then he curses quietly. "That Hunter . . ."

"Yeah." I clasp my hands around the glass, and we sit in silence together. For the first time since I've been alone with Vin, I don't feel uncomfortable. The silence is actually nice, like a warm, comforting blanket.

I feel relieved now that I've told him everything, as if a weight has lifted from my shoulders. I've been walking around with this for months.

I'm just about to take a sip of water when the silence is broken by a bloodcurdling scream from outside.

Got her.

LOTUS

"Nova!" My voice echoes through the trees. Spot runs with me. Vin is just behind us.

What happened? That scream must have been Nova. Is she hurt?

"Nova, Nova, Nova!" Vin's voice is like a siren.

"Quiet!" I grip his arm and listen. Somewhere in the distance, someone's wailing.

"There!"

We run together, toward the sound.

We're coming, I think. *Hang in there just a little longer.*

And then I see Nova sitting on the ground, her hands around her ankle.

"Nova?"

Nova turns to look. As soon as she sees me, her eyes go from terrified to vicious. "This is *your* fault!"

"What?" I take a few steps forward. "What's . . ."

In the middle of my sentence, I fall silent. Nova's right foot is caught in a bear trap. The metal has pierced her leather shoe, and there's bright-red blood on the iron teeth.

"Nova . . ." I kneel down and pull Spot away from her. "Let me help you."

"Don't you dare," Nova shrieks hysterically. "If you touch it, I'll kill you."

"That trap needs to be opened," I say. "Then your foot can come out."

"Are you crazy or something?" Nova looks wide-eyed at Vin, who just nods.

"Lotus is right."

"Call an ambulance." Nova looks at me, more tears welling up in her eyes. "You have a phone, don't you?"

I take my phone out of my pocket, but I see the problem right away. "No signal. I have to go back to the house!"

Nova groans.

"We'll carry you back there, but first we have to get your foot out of this."

"You've got no idea how to open the thing!" Nova's eyes are shooting fire. For a moment, I see her as she was by the bike rack, months ago. She stuck the knife into that bike tire so hard that it was as if it wasn't the tire, but the bike's owner she was stabbing.

Something crackles inside my head, like a faulty

fluorescent tube. Those bike tires . . . As I stare at the bear trap clamped around Nova's foot, the information inside my head starts to slot together.

What if . . .

"Lotus!" Vin is looking at me. "Just do it!"

"Yes . . ." I force myself to focus. "I'll count to three and then I'll open it. One . . ."

"If you mess this up, I *will* kill you," hisses Nova.

"Two . . ."

"It hurts so much . . ."

"Three."

I grab the trap and pull with all my might. There's so much tension on the metal that my fingers cramp. The trap opens slightly before shooting out of my hands.

The bang echoes through my head, followed by another scream from Nova.

"What are you doing?!" Vin yells at me, his face bright red.

"Sorry . . ." I look at Nova, who has curled up on the ground. Her lips are so tightly pressed together that her mouth is just a white line.

"Sorry," I repeat. "I'll try again."

"No," says Vin. "I'll do it."

Without counting to three, he pulls the trap open. I take hold of Nova's leg and pull her foot out. She does not make another sound. Not even when Vin picks her up and carries her all the way to the house.

I walk a few yards behind them. Nova's hair is hanging down like a curtain.

Again, those flat bike tires flash through my mind. What if I'm right? What if Unknown is who I think they are?

There's a bitter taste in my mouth, which I can barely swallow away.

When we finally see the red roof tiles of the farmhouse, my phone rings. Three short buzzes. I'm back in range.

Vin turns around. "What is it?"

I don't answer, my eyes shooting over the lines.

> In the garage there's a red first-aid box with some antibiotics. Make sure she takes the pills, or the wounds will get infected.

It's clear: that trap wasn't left by a hunter. It was there because Unknown wanted one of us to step on it.

I look up, straight into Vin's worried eyes.

"Lotus?" Vin lowers Nova a little. "What is it?"

Then another message arrives.

> I'm going to make sure the whole story gets out if you call for help. After all, I had to do everything all by myself.

"Lotus!" Vin sounds furious. "What does it say?!"

I can't answer. Images of the past year are flashing through my mind like a badly edited movie.

Now I know who Unknown is.

"Take Nova inside." My voice comes from far away. "I'll follow in a minute."

Luckily, Vin doesn't ask any more questions when I head for the garage.

I shove the lawn mower out of the way and search the shelves. A bright red first-aid kit should stand out, shouldn't it?

And then I spot something red on the bottom shelf. When I pull it out, a couple of cans of paint fall from the shelves above me. I leave them on the ground and head into the house, where Vin has put Nova on the couch. Spot is nervously winding around me, quietly whimpering with his tail hanging low.

"Not now, boy." I hurry to Nova. She's deathly pale and her eyes are closed. She looks like a corpse.

"Is she conscious?" I ask Vin.

"Of course I am," growls Nova, opening her eyes. "Have you called the ambulance?"

"I have a first-aid kit," I say to Vin. "Nova, I need to take off your shoe."

I click the box open and see some ointment, several kinds of bandages, painkillers, Band-Aids, antiseptic wipes, and a . . . container of pills. Those must be the antibiotics.

"Lotus, hurry." Vin's forceful voice brings me back to the living room. I look at the contents of the first-aid box again. Where to begin? Spot once had a shard of glass in his foot. When we came back from a walk, I saw blood on the floor in the hallway. I managed to take the glass out myself and patch him up. The vet was really pleased with me for acting so quickly and doing a good job.

So I do exactly the same thing now: I jump into action. It's as if a switch inside my head flicks and a different Lotus takes over.

"Untie the laces and take off the shoe," I say to Vin, who seems glad that he doesn't have to think for himself. As soon as he starts tugging on Nova's shoe, she clenches her jaw. Tears are streaming down her cheeks, and her yellow sock is soaked with blood. Without hesitating, I take off her sock—and I see the three wounds in her flesh.

I put on gloves and clean the cuts with an antiseptic wipe. Nova makes a strange sound but doesn't say anything.

Do the wounds need stitching? I rummage around in the box and take out the Band-Aids. Perfect. I open the packet and pinch the skin around the wounds. When the dressings are on all three of the wounds, the bleeding stops almost immediately.

Strangely, the wounds don't seem as deep as I'd feared.

Nova's leather army shoes absorbed much of the damage. I'm suddenly happy with Romy's rugged taste in clothes. I don't want to imagine what might have happened if Nova had been wearing flip-flops.

I clean off the last of the blood with another wipe and grab a large bandage, which I wrap around Nova's foot.

I raise Nova's leg and put a big cushion under her foot and then look at the final result.

"Is that enough, do you think?" Vin says, placing his hand on Nova's sweaty forehead.

"I hope so." I point at her foot. "That needs to remain elevated."

"Call that ambulance," Nova says weakly.

"Yes." I look at Vin. "Will you come with me for a second?"

Vin takes his hand off Nova's forehead and gives her a kiss. "Help is on the way. Okay?"

I lead Vin into the kitchen and take out my phone.

"Let me do it," says Vin as I struggle to open the flap. My body has only just started to react. My hands are trembling uncontrollably.

"You got another message, didn't you?" Vin runs his eyes over the words. When he's finished reading, he looks at me. I see a mixture of disgust and disbelief in his eyes.

"That trap was left there *on purpose*?"

"Yes. But do you know who by?"

"No?"

Well, I do know. Why didn't I see it sooner? But it was so obvious that I simply overlooked it. Like when you're searching for your keys and then realize you were holding them all along.

"It's Robin," I say. "Robin Schild."

FALL

I took a deep breath and knocked three times.

"Robin?" Reid Hunter looked up from his test papers when I entered his classroom. "What can I do for you?"

The words tumbled through my head like autumn leaves.

Where to begin?

I didn't know where to look.

"Why don't you just sit down for a moment? Did something happen in class today?"

I shook my head. "Not just today."

"What's up?"

"They're tearing me to shreds."

Reid Hunter leaned back in his chair and steepled his fingers.

"Who is?"

"Nova, Vin, and Lotus."

Reid Hunter frowned. "Are you sure about that?"

What kind of question was that?

Of course I was sure!

"I'll talk to them." Reid Hunter's expression became slightly softer. "It'll be okay."

On Wednesday, after the last lesson, Bittersweet walked up to me.

"I've come to apologize."

I couldn't believe my ears.

Her voice sounded different.

Calmer.

Almost friendly.

"Hello? I just said sorry. It won't happen again."

"Yes," I managed to say. "Okay."

"Well, you're in a good mood."

My dad came into the garden, where I was singing as I swept up the leaves.

The two toffees in my mouth had almost melted away.

Two days had gone by since Bittersweet's apology and she'd kept her word.

I'd barely seen the three of them.

They really were leaving me alone.

Things were finally going to get better.

I was going to buy Reid Hunter a big box of chocolates to say thank you.

Or maybe I could take him some cuttings for his vegetable garden.

"This was in the mail, by the way."

My dad handed me a white envelope with my name on it.

I leaned my rake against the wall and opened the envelope.

When I read what was inside, the last bits of toffee slipped down my throat like a bitter pill.

```
Not a good idea to rat on us to RH.

But wouldn't you know it? Lotus
happens to be his favorite student.

One more word and we know where to
                find you.

From now on, you'll have to do
    everything all by yourself.
```

LOTUS

"Y-you think Robin's the one who's sending these messages?" Vin stammers. He now looks just as pale as Nova. "Why on earth would you think that?"

"Read that sentence!" I jab my index finger at the screen. " 'I had to do everything all by myself.' "

Robin was in the woods that night, she destroyed our tires, and now she's come for Nova.

How could I be so stupid to think this was just about me? She hates all three of us.

"I don't get it." Vin looks at me. "How did she get this number? You said yourself that you only had this phone to talk to Mr. Hunter."

I think for a moment.

"From Reid," I say. "The two of them must have kept in touch after she left the school."

Reid always had a soft spot for Robin. That was clear

from the start. He took her under his wing, like she was some kind of shelter animal. I hated it.

At the beginning of this year, when Reid came to me because Robin had told him that we were tearing her to shreds, he looked at me with such disappointment that I had no choice but to deny it outright. I didn't want him ever to look at me like that again.

So we got off with a warning, but from that moment, it was no-holds-barred for me and Nova. We had an extra reason to hate Robin.

"But if it really is her . . ." Vin shakes his head. "I'm going crazy."

"What are you two whispering about?" Nova calls from the couch. "Where's the ambulance?"

I look at her.

"We have to tell her."

"Are you serious?" Vin seems to wake up suddenly. "We don't know anything for sure yet! Do you want to make her panic?"

"So, what are we supposed to do? She thinks we're calling an ambulance!"

Vin brushes the hair out of his face. "I'll come up with something to occupy her. And that'll give you some time."

"To do what?"

"Try to contact Robin." Vin points at my phone. "Ask her what she wants. Maybe we can get her to leave us alone."

"Do you think I haven't tried that already? She won't answer!"

"Then think of something else," Vin says, looking me straight in the eyes. "I'll make sure Nova takes those antibiotics and painkillers. Just go."

I slump down onto the ground outside the front door. My thumbs hover above the keys of my phone. What if it all goes wrong again? The last time I sent Unknown a message, she snuck into our house in the middle of the night!

What if I make it even worse?

But then I remember Nova's foot in the trap. What's next? Is Robin planning to murder us?

Vin is right. We have to figure out what she wants.

> Robin? We'd like to talk to you.

I don't know if this is going to work, but it's a start. When she reads this message, she won't know what hit her. I'm sure she didn't mean to give away her identity.

I try to picture Robin's face, but strangely it remains vague, like a blurred photo.

Since she left school, it's like I've erased her from my memory. I was so happy we were rid of her and that I didn't have to lie to Reid anymore.

I'd have liked to tell him the truth, but I don't know if he would have taken our side. Robin seemed important to him in some weird kind of way, maybe even as important as me.

I wait for the buzz in my hand, but my phone stays silent.

I stare at the trees in front of me. If it really is Robin who is watching us, how did she know we were coming here?

Did Reid tell her? Nova might've told him in class where the farmhouse was, even though she wouldn't tell me.

There's only one way to find out. . . .

Feeling sick in the pit of my stomach, I open our chat history. My last words to Reid are still unanswered at the bottom.

We need to stop doing this. It's getting too dangerous. x

I close the phone.

No, I am *not* going to call him.

But what am I going to do? Do I have to go back in there and confess to Vin that I haven't made any progress at all?

This isn't about Reid and me. I have to do this for Nova, for our safety.

I open up the phone again and press Reid's number. How many times in the past year have we talked secretly on this phone? But I never called him. It was always the other way around. I obviously had no way of knowing when his wife was around.

The phone rings, the sound penetrating deep into my brain. With every ring, I think about Karen, who must be on school vacation now too. Reid told me they met during teacher training and that she teaches English at a different school. I don't know much more than that. Reid preferred not to talk about her when he was with me. And to be honest, that was fine by me.

"Yes?"

The sudden sound of his voice startles me.

"Reid?" My voice is suddenly trembling like mad. "I-it's me."

"I know." He sounds impatient. "What do you want?"

He must be mad about the message I sent.

"Sorry," I say. "Sorry I sent you that message the other day. Sorry I'm calling you now."

"It's okay." He lets out a sigh and then his voice sounds a lot warmer. "How are things going at Nerd Central? That's what Nova called it, isn't it?"

Reality hits me again.

"Fine," I croak. "I was just wondering . . . Did you tell anyone where we were going?"

"What do you mean? Who would I have told?"

"Robin?" I almost whisper her name.

"Robin?" Reid repeats. He sounds surprised. "Where did you get that idea?"

"Are you still in touch with her?"

"Um . . . now and then. I might have mentioned the farmhouse a while ago, but what does that matter?"

So Robin knew because of him. . . . I lower the phone a couple of inches.

"Lo? Is everything okay?" Reid's voice is coming from a long way off.

A remote farmhouse.

A lockdown.

We made it really easy for Robin.

"Lotus? Are you still there?"

"Yes." I raise the phone to my ear again. "Yes, I'm still here. Everything's fine."

I want Reid to see through it, for him to keep asking until I tell him the truth. But it's just like when he asked me if it was true about what we were doing to Robin. He hears what he wants to hear.

No, I don't know what Robin's talking about. We might have made a joke that she took the wrong way, but that was seriously all it was.

"Glad to hear everything's going well. Hang on . . . Karen?" A hand is placed over the phone, and I hear a muffled woman's voice in the background. When Reid starts talking again, his voice sounds like it does at school: friendly but professional. "Yes, I'm back again, Mr. van Dijk. I'll send the lists ASAP. Have a good day."

And then the line goes dead.

* * *

When I go back inside, Nova is asleep. Spot is lying beside her like a guard dog, and he looks up when he hears me.

"She took the pills," says Vin. "Did you speak to Robin?"

I shake my head. "Reid. He told Robin where we were going. The two of them were still in touch. . . ."

"Really?"

"Apparently." I look at Nova, who is sleeping deeply. "Come on."

"What are we going to do?" Vin asks.

"Robin must be hiding somewhere in the forest. If we find her, we can confront her."

Vin's face falls. "You want to go to her? I don't know if I . . ."

"There are two of us." I look at him. Since we got to West Virginia, there's been no sign of the laid-back Vin I know. "Or would you rather wait here until she comes up with another idea to torment us?"

"Of course not," says Vin irritably. "But we can't leave Nova on her own here, can we?"

"Spot is with her," I say, even though I know that Spot wouldn't do anything except growl and bark a bit. He makes a load of noise, but when it comes down to it, he wouldn't hurt a fly. He proved as much last night.

"Anyway, you could fire a cannon when Nova's fast asleep."

Vin nods.

"Hey, don't worry. We'll be back in no time."

Vin leans over Nova and plants a long kiss on her fore-head. It's such a loving gesture that I feel like I'm disturb-ing an intimate moment.

"Come on," I say again. "We need to hurry."

"Where should we begin?" Vin says, looking around. "All I see are trees."

"We'll start where the bear trap was. If Robin put it there, there's a reason she chose that place."

"Just don't go stepping on one." Vin shudders. "I bet there are more out there."

He's probably right. Robin won't have set just one trap. Then there wouldn't have been much chance of Nova stepping on it.

The forest suddenly feels like a minefield. With every step, I pay close attention to where I'm putting my foot.

"Here!" Vin's voice catches in his throat. "Look . . ."

As I get closer, I see a whole line of traps, well hidden among the leaves. It's a semicircle, extending deep into the forest.

"R-Robin is really disturbed . . . ," I stammer.

Vin gasps. "Where did she get those things from?"

"No idea, but we need to keep going."

"Are you sure?" Vin sounds short of breath. "She's clearly prepared. Shouldn't we arm ourselves?"

"With what? A kitchen knife?"

Vin chuckles nervously. "Or a solar-powered light?"

"We're just going to take a look," I say. "We'll be back soon."

I try not to look at the sharp teeth of the trap as I take a big step over it. Nova must have been in so much pain. She said it felt like she was dying, and I believe her.

Nova isn't someone who makes a fuss. One time at elementary school, she fell on her wrist and she didn't even flinch. She refused to even tell the teacher. She lived with the pain for ages, until her mom finally realized she was hurt and took her to see the doctor. At the hospital, they discovered she had a minor fracture.

Vin and I walk deeper and deeper into the forest. The vegetation here is denser, and it's almost as if the sun doesn't dare to enter.

Something rustles nearby. I peer into the undergrowth, but I don't see anything moving. I feel like a wild animal that could be shot at any moment.

"How about we just go back?" I suggest.

Vin breathes a sigh of relief. "Yes, please."

Just as I'm about to turn around, I see something at my feet. A wave of shock goes through me when I realize what it is.

"Vin . . . ," I gasp. "Look."

FALL

"Do you think it's happening again?"

I heard my parents talking in the living room. They didn't realize I was downstairs too.

"Why do you think that?" my dad asked.

"Because she's putting on weight," my mom said. "And that's what always happens."

I clenched my teeth.

"Why do things keep going so badly?" my dad said with a deep sigh. "Should we have tried to make her more resilient?"

"Maybe," I heard my mom say.

That weekend, the doorbell rang.

"Robin, can you get that?" my mom called from the kitchen.

What if Bittersweet had sent another delivery guy?

I couldn't afford that many pizzas!

But when I opened the door, a man in a button-down shirt and rimless glasses was standing there.

He looked at me with a smile.

"Robin?"

"Yes?" I looked over my shoulder, but my mom was still in the kitchen. "Who are you?"

"I'm here to see you." The man ran his eyes over me. "I'm interested."

"Sorry?"

"In a quickie."

"Sorry?" My head just about exploded. "What are you talking about?"

"The advert," he said. "The one with the photo of you. Although you do look different. How old are you actually?"

Bittersweet.

What had she gone and done this time?

"Fifty dollars," said the man, taking a crumpled bill from his pocket. "That's how much it costs, isn't it?"

I slammed the door in his face.

"Who was it?" called my mom.

"No one."

My parents wanted me to be more resilient.

From now on, I really was on my own.

* * *

"Robin, you're already here." Reid Hunter finally came around the corner with a stack of paper in his hands. "Sorry I'm late. A student had detention."

One of his shirt buttons was done up wrong.

He saw me looking and quickly fixed it.

"What did you want to talk to me about?"

"I wanted to thank you for your help," I heard myself saying. "The bullying has stopped."

LOTUS

"Toffees . . ."

Vin looks wide-eyed at the wrapper in my hand. "Those were her favorites."

I nod. I always remember Robin with those empty toffee wrappers on her desk. Nova and I sometimes saw her get through an entire bag of them. Her teeth just kept on grinding away, like there was no stopping her.

I look at the empty wrapper in my hand. One piece of paper, but it's like we just found Robin's ID. Now I'm a hundred percent certain that it's her.

Nova is still sleeping. I sigh with relief when I see her chest calmly moving up and down.

"Well guarded, boy." I rest my hand on Spot's head, and he wags his tail enthusiastically.

The coffee table creaks under my weight when I sit on it. When Nova is asleep, she seems younger. Her face becomes softer, as if someone has erased her sharp features. She's even snoring a little.

"I locked all the doors," says Vin.

I look around. When we got here, all those windows made the room feel nice and light, but now it feels as if we're sitting inside a huge glass box.

"Should we call Romy?" I ask.

I think about Nova's sister, who'll drive straight here, tires screeching. I promised her that I'd look after her little sister, and less than twenty-four hours later she stepped on a bear trap.

"You really want Romy to come here?" asks Vin, as if he can read my mind.

"No, not really," I say quietly. "She'll be furious when she hears what happened to Nova's foot."

"Who'll be furious?" Nova opens her eyes. She tries to turn onto her side, but then groans. "Ow . . ."

"Just lie there," I say quickly. "You stepped on a bear trap, remember?"

"I'm not senile."

In spite of everything, I feel a smile spread on my lips. Even in the middle of the storm, Nova is still herself.

"Lotus and I have found something," says Vin. "But you have to promise us you're not going to flip."

Nova looks around. "Flip? What do you mean? Where's the ambulance?"

My stomach is churning. She trusted me. She thinks help is on the way.

"We didn't call an ambulance," I say quietly.

Nova's eyes shoot in Vin's direction. "What?!"

"It wasn't an accident." Vin points at her foot. "Someone left that trap there for you."

Nova frowns. "What?!" she yells for the second time.

Now there's no way back. We have to tell her everything. She needs to know that Robin is behind this.

"The person who's threatening me also set the bear traps," I say quietly. "It was deliberate."

"But . . . what do I have to do with this? I'm not the one who's hooking up with Reid Hunter!"

"This isn't about Reid."

"Then who is it about?"

"It was Robin who set those traps." Vin gets straight to the point.

A moment of silence.

"Who?"

For a second, I think Nova seriously doesn't remember who we're talking about, but then she gets up off the couch on one leg, tears of pain welling in her eyes.

"Nova . . . ?" I say cautiously.

"No." Nova shakes her head. "No, no, no. That bitch doesn't exist anymore."

"It's her," says Vin. "Lotus, show her the wrapper."

I take the toffee paper out of my pocket. "We found this by the bear traps. She's hiding somewhere in the forest, but we didn't dare to go any farther without you knowing where we were."

Nova stares at my hand as if I'm holding a tarantula in front of her nose.

"Robin gave herself away with her last message." I take out my phone. "She said we weren't allowed to call for help, that she had to do everything on her own too. Those were exactly the words we used in that letter we sent her."

"No." Nova knocks my phone away. "Robin left the school. She's gone, disappeared."

I know just how Nova feels. Didn't I think the same? We were rid of her. She had finally exited the stage. How could we know she'd come back for an encore?

Nova turns and tries to hop away. "I am not going to be a part of this."

"Where are you going?" I ask.

"To pack my bags. I'm calling Romy and she'll come get us. If you guys don't want to come, fine, but I'm not staying here another second."

"Nova, listen. She says we can't call for help," says Vin.

"IT IS NOT ROBIN!"

"Think about it. . . ." I look around me. "Somehow, Robin knows this house. She knew there would be a welcome package. She even left antibiotics in the garage because she knew one of us would step on that bear trap. She planned all of this—get that into your head! This isn't some spur-of-the-moment kind of thing. If we go running around like headless chickens and call your sister . . ."

"What did you say?" Nova's eyes flash to the small bottle on the coffee table. "Are those *her* pills?"

"Y-yes."

"You guys gave me *her* pills?!" Nova's voice cracks. "Who knows what's in them?!"

"There's nothing in them," I say quickly, but I feel my hands starting to sweat. We didn't even stop to think that Robin might have messed with the pills.

"You guys have gone crazy!" Nova slowly stumbles backward until she bumps into the small table in the corner. The old-fashioned yellow telephone almost falls onto the floor when she grabs the receiver.

"What are you going to do?"

"I'm calling my sister." Nova looks at me so fiercely that I feel like I'm being strangled. "And you guys are not going to stop me."

I look at Vin, but he can't move either.

Nova dials a number, her taps on the keypad sounding like hammer blows.

She can't. Vin is right: if Robin finds out that we're involving Romy, I'm sure it's going to end in disaster.

Another digit, and another. I count them in my head. One more and it'll start ringing.

But then there's a brief crackle, followed by a curse from Nova. She drops the receiver as if it's on fire.

"What the . . ."

Vin jumps up. "What is it?"

"It . . ." Nova gapes at the receiver, which is lying at her feet. "It shocked me!"

"How is that possible?"

"That thing is electrified!" Nova limps past us. I hold out my hand to her, but she pushes it away and stumbles upstairs.

When I bend to pick up the receiver, Vin stops me.

"Don't!"

I pull my sleeve over my hand and cautiously touch the receiver. Nothing happens. It's a perfectly normal receiver.

"I picked it up yesterday too," I say. "All I heard was the dial tone. Listen."

I hold it to Vin's ear. When he realizes that I'm right, he frowns.

"But how?"

"We get a shock if we use it." I can hear for myself how bizarre it sounds. "That way, we stay in lockdown."

"And what about your phone?" Vin says, pointing at it.

"I wasn't supposed to bring it."

"Do you think that made Robin angry?" asks Vin.

"Maybe," I reply.

I try to picture an angry Robin. What would that look

like? In all those months, she never fought back. Sometimes I wanted her to get mad, but she just kept acting like a puppy, with those big, scared eyes. All that time, she remained the victim.

"Nova?"

I push down the door handle and see her lying on the bed, with her back to the door. Her suitcase is open beside her, but she hasn't started packing yet.

"Fuck off," she snarls.

"I'm sorry," I say, carefully sitting down on the corner of the mattress.

"What for?" comes her muffled voice.

"A thousand things. I should never have given you those pills. You're absolutely right. And I should have been honest with you about Reid, but he thought it was better to keep it secret."

"I'm your best friend." Nova turns around, her face wet with tears. "Does that mean nothing to you?"

"It means everything! I was terrified just now. When you were lying there bleeding on the couch, I felt so guilty."

Nova just stares at me. What if she doesn't forgive me? I try to imagine a life without Nova, but I can't. She's always there. We are each other's shadows, conjoined twins with no blood ties.

"So it's Robin," Nova says quietly.

"Yes." I'm whispering too. Is Nova thinking about that Monday after the school dance? We waited for Robin at the entrance, but she didn't turn up. That afternoon we went to her house, but no one came to the door. The curtains were closed; there was no sign of life. She didn't show her face in the days that followed either. Reid eventually told our class that she wasn't coming back.

"What now?" asks Nova.

"I sent a message asking her if she'll talk to us, but she hasn't answered." I can hear now how lame it sounds. If I were Robin, I wouldn't answer either.

I point at Nova's hand. "Did that receiver really give you a shock?"

"It was like touching an electric fence." Nova makes a face.

"But how did she manage to do that?"

"No idea, but she was a huge nerd. Maybe she found a tutorial on the internet?" I look around. "Do you think this place belongs to her family or something?"

"No," says Nova. "I just think she got here before us. That meant she had all the time she needed to prepare."

I picture Robin scurrying around the house. Was that when she punctured the mountain bike's tire and left the first-aid kit? It's a logical explanation. The owner isn't going to check the bike tires every time. They automatically get complaints when something isn't working one hundred percent.

"Maybe she slept in this bed. . . ." Nova winces as she looks at the mattress. "I want to go home."

"Me too," I say.

"Where's Vin?"

"Downstairs. He's really worried about you."

"Good."

"You need to talk with him, Nova. Just ask him what's going on."

"I'm scared of the answer." Nova groans quietly as she shifts position.

"Is it really painful?"

"Robin's miracle pills don't work."

"Want me to get you an extra Tylenol? I have some in my toiletry bag."

"No, I don't want to be here on my own." Nova closes her eyes, and another tear escapes from the corner of her eye. "Shit, Lotus, if it really is Robin, then . . ."

She doesn't finish her sentence, but I know what she wants to say. Robin will destroy us.

"How does she know we're here?" Nova asks.

"Because of Reid. I called him and he admitted that he told Robin about the farmhouse."

"So, the two of them are still in touch?" Nova's face clouds over. "You don't think the two of them were . . . ?"

"Of course not," I say, but I hear the doubt in my voice. The thought has certainly occurred to me—quite a few times, in fact.

My phone buzzes three times. Startled, Nova looks up.
"Is it her?"
I flip it open and nod.
"Show me."
I run my eyes over the words and feel Nova tugging my arm. "Lotus?"

It doesn't matter who I am. This isn't a whodunit. This is a what's next.

FALL

"Robin." Reid Hunter shouted my name down the hall. "Just the person I wanted to see! I wanted to ask if you'll help out on the dance committee."

"Can't . . . can't someone else do it?"

Reid Hunter laughs. "I'm sure they can, but I want you."

"That's nearly everyone." Reid Hunter looked around the group.

The dance committee was made up of teachers and students, who were all sitting together.

On the table, there was coffee, tea, and cookies.

I'd already had two cookies.

So far, everything was going well.

No one had asked what I was doing there.

But then the door opened.

I heard her voice before I saw her.

"Sorry I'm late."

All eyes were on the girl who came in.

Not only was she late, but she was also stunning.

And she was Bittersweet's sidekick.

"I want to leave the committee."

Reid Hunter looked at me in amazement. "Why?"

"It's not my kind of thing."

"But I thought you had great ideas. A masked ball—where did you get that idea from?"

"A movie," I said. "But I want to quit."

"Is it because of Lotus?"

The question hit me like a sledgehammer.

Had Reid Hunter noticed that I hadn't said another word after she got there?

I weighed my options.

If I told the truth, Mom and Dad would find out about what was going on at school.

They'd hear about that pervert who came to our house.

And Bittersweet?

I wouldn't be safe for another second.

"No," I said. "Not because of Lotus."

"That's good, because Lotus didn't join the committee because of you, if that's what you're worried about."

I looked at him.

"Then why'd she join?"

To my surprise, Reid Hunter blushed a bit.

I'd never seen him do that before.

LOTUS

"What's next?" Vin looks up from the message and at Nova and me. We're sitting downstairs on the couches, and Spot is lying in a strip of sunlight on the floor. "Or who?"

"Stop scaring me," I say.

"But it's true, isn't it?" Vin counts on one finger. "You were the first. She snuck into your bedroom and sent you those messages." He adds a second finger. "Then Nova stepped on that bear trap. *Who's* next?"

I'm terrified at the thought of Robin taking us out one by one. Are we supposed to just sit here and wait until she gets to Vin?

"We have to go home," I say. "Let's call a taxi. It can take us into town and then Romy can fetch us from there."

I try not to think about how Nova's sister will react.

Nova nods. "I'll use your phone to let her know we want to go home."

"And then?" Vin says. "Robin says we're not allowed to get help, that we have to do everything all by ourselves. What do you think she'll do when she hears we've left? She'll go wild! She'll tell everyone what happened."

"So, what are we going to do?" I yell.

Vin shifts his position. "Robin is clearly not going to respond to our suggestion that we should talk, so we need to lure her out of her hiding place some other way."

Nova looks at him. "And how do you plan to do that?"

"With something that's important to her," I say. I think about it. What do we actually know about Robin?

"Plants," says Vin. "She was always talking about her garden, wasn't she?"

I nod. "I'd completely forgotten about that. I remember her at school once, bragging about how she knew the names of all the plants."

"Her mom and dad . . . ," Nova says slowly. "If we kidnap them, she'll give in right away."

No one laughs. I look at the old-fashioned telephone, which is back on the table. Robin doesn't just know a lot about plants. She clearly knew how to electrify a telephone too. I underestimated her. I always thought she was a defenseless victim, but that's not what she is at all. Or at least she's not anymore.

She's prepared—down to the last detail. On her own? Or did someone help her?

I think about Robin's dad, who once caught us writing

on her car outside their front door. None of us saw him coming. He was suddenly standing behind us. He grabbed Nova by her jacket and raised his fist. I saw the fury in his eyes. I think he really wanted to hit her.

But then he suddenly let her go, and the three of us made a run for it.

Nova said later that it looked like he was shocked by his own aggression, but I think it was something else. Maybe the guy knew that his daughter could handle it herself. Because she'd already come up with her plan.

Maybe he helped her with everything.

I bury my face in my hands. Why did Reid have to be so dumb and shoot his mouth off? He should never have told Robin about the farmhouse, and then we'd . . .

"Reid . . ." I look up.

Vin frowns. "What about him?"

"Something that's important to her." I repeat my own words.

"Or *someone.*"

"What do you mean?" Nova asks.

I stand up and walk back and forth. The plan is unfolding inside my head like a complicated piece of origami.

"Reid's the one we want. . . ."

"Just quit it with that secret language of yours!" Nova throws a cushion at me. "What are you trying to say?"

I stop pacing. "We have to get Reid to come here."

Nova's jaw drops. Vin's face clouds over.

"The two of them had a connection," I continue. "You guys saw it, too, right?"

"We're not supposed to get help," Vin says again.

"We have to," I say.

"It's an insane plan." Vin shakes his head furiously. "There's no way we're going to do this. Then you'll have to confess everything to Reid. Is that what you want?"

Far from it. I can already picture Reid's face when I tell him the truth about Robin. The whole truth, including about the school dance . . .

"We have no choice," I say. "Robin won't talk to us, but maybe she'll talk to Reid."

"And how are you going to get him to come all the way here on his vacation?" Nova looks at me. "Do you think he's going to make a fun weekend of it with his wife?"

Karen. The woman I've seen only once, when I bumped into her and Reid in town. She was walking so close to him that she just about disappeared into him. I followed them for some time, but eventually I went home.

"I have a plan." At the thought of having to call Reid again, my stomach does a flip.

"I'm not sure . . . ," Nova says.

"I am." Vin stands up. "You leave that man out of it."

I look at him. "Sorry?"

"If Reid finds out about everything that happened, we'll be thrown out of school. Bye exams, bye graduation . . ."

I feel irritation bubbling up inside me. Vin has plenty

to say, but he isn't coming up with any solutions. Do I have to think of everything myself?

"What do you care?" I snap at him. "You want to go traveling. You can do that without graduating."

"And what about you?" Vin grabs me by the wrists. "You want to study veterinary medicine. Do you really want to have to repeat a year at another school? Maybe no other schools will even accept us as students when they know what we've done!"

I look at Nova, who is watching from the couch.

"Vin's right," she says.

I give a deep sigh. "Nova . . ."

"But so are you," Nova adds. "I don't want to think about what Robin will do if Reid Hunter comes here, but you're right: we need his help."

The phone rings. Twice, three times.

"You think he's going to answer?" Nova looks at me anxiously. The phone is between us on the couch, with the speaker on. Vin has taken Spot for a pee outside the front door. He doesn't want anything to do with this.

"I think he . . ." Before I can finish my sentence, I hear Reid's voice for the second time today.

"Hello?"

"Reid, it's me."

"Why are you calling? I'm at home, Lo."

"*Lo?*" Nova giggles nervously and claps her hand over her mouth.

"There's something I have to tell you." My heart is pounding so hard that it hurts. "Do you have a moment?"

"Karen's out shopping, but she could come back any minute."

"Nova and Vin know."

There's silence. For a moment, I think Reid's hung up, but then I hear his voice again. It sounds a bit shaky.

"What the hell have you done?"

"I had to tell them." I take a deep breath. The tears in my voice can be clearly heard when I add: "I don't want to keep it a secret anymore."

"But . . ."

I can picture Reid standing in his living room, one hand holding his phone, the other clawing at his curls.

". . . but we had a deal!"

A *deal*, like I'm his business partner.

"I can't keep it up anymore."

"We'll talk about it when you're back, okay? We'll think of something, I promise."

Nova gives me a nudge. I know what sentence needs to come next, but I'd rather not go there.

"I'm going to tell your wife."

This time, the silence is a short one.

"No, you're not."

"I don't have a choice, Reid!" My voice sounds thick, as if my heart is trying to escape through my throat.

"Calm down . . ."

"Hunter, that's her last name now, right? Yeah, of course. You got married."

"What are you talking about?" Reid sounds really panicky now. "This isn't like you. Please, just tell me what I can do to stop you."

"Nothing."

"Of course there's something. Do you want to go away together for the night? How about that nice hotel by the beach, the one you were talking about the other day?"

The suck-up tone of his voice makes me nauseous. He never wanted to go to a hotel with me. I suggested it so many times that I lost count. But we always stayed safely within the four walls of his classroom, with the doors locked and the blinds down. So, how come it's suddenly possible now?

"No."

"Then what do you want?"

"I want you to come here."

Another silence.

"To the farmhouse?"

"Yes."

"You have lost the plot."

"You asked what I wanted."

"He's not going to do it," Nova whispers in my ear. I'm

afraid she's right. What are we going to do if Reid doesn't cooperate? How are we going to get Robin to stop?

But then I hear Reid's voice again. "Tomorrow, okay? I'll have to come up with some excuse and then tomorrow morning I'll drive out to you guys."

I pick the phone up off the couch.

"Good," I say.

"Just don't say anything to Karen, please. We'll figure this out, Lo. I—"

In the middle of his sentence, I flip the phone shut. I breathe out.

Nova just stares at me. "Wow, *Lo* . . ."

"Shut up." I feel tears burning in my eyes.

"Sorry." Nova puts her arms around me and gives me a hug. "I'm sorry that you had to do that."

I hold her tight. Nova whispers words into my hair. I clench my jaw.

The things I just said to Reid—I'll never be able to make it up to him. I knew what a risk he was taking with me. I'm still a minor. If what happened between us ever gets out, I'm sure my mom and dad will take him to court. They'll say he's a creep who abused his position.

He was a nice teacher, but when I was alone with him, he was totally amazing. He talked about his work with such passion, and I knew how that felt. I've known ever since I was little that I wanted to be a vet. And then there was the way Reid looked at me, like I was his favorite person in the whole world. The sparkle in his eyes before he kissed me, as if he couldn't wait a second longer. And every time, over and over again. With him, each kiss felt like the first one. But the second I mentioned his wife, it was like none of that ever happened.

Nova lets go of me. "But hey, good news—it worked. He's coming here."

"Yeah." I know she's right: that was the goal. So why does it feel like I've lost?

"It's really weird. He sounds so different than he does at school," says Nova. "Much younger."

"Well, he *is* young."

Nova raises an eyebrow, and I burst out laughing.

"Okay, then not old, old."

"I don't get you." Nova shakes her head.

"I don't want to talk about it anymore."

"Oh, I bet you do." Nova slides closer to me. For a moment, it's like when we were twelve and she found out I'd kissed a boy from another class.

"You are going to tell me *everything*. I want to know how he kisses, how you seduced him—"

"He seduced me!" I shout. "Why do you guys think it was me who started it? Vin said the same."

"Hey, where is Vin, anyway?" Nova looks around. "He was just taking Spot for a pee, wasn't he?"

I walk over to the window, but I don't see anyone. I go into the hall and open the front door. "Vin?"

Maybe he's behind the house and can't hear me.

"Vin!" This time my voice rings through the trees. "Where are you?"

No response.

I walk out into the sunlight, but there's no sign of any-one. The forest is as quiet as ever.

What Vin said is echoing inside my head: *What's next? Or who?*

I spin on my axis. "Vin!"

Nova appears in the doorway behind me, her injured foot hovering above the mat.

"Nova . . ." I hardly dare to look at her. "I think he's gone."

LOTUS

"Hey, be quiet for a second, will you?" Nova sticks her finger in the air. "I think I heard something."

I listen carefully and then I hear what she means. A quiet whimpering.

"Spot!" I run toward the sound, all the way around the house. Spot is sitting by the woodpile. He pulls the leash taut as soon as he sees me.

Then I see the other end of the leash around Vin's wrist. He's lying on his stomach, with his face turned to one side. His eyes are closed.

It's like I'm watching a movie and there's a scene with some walker finding a dead body. But this time I'm the walker and the dead body is my friend's.

"Vin . . ." Nova limps past me and kneels down. When she starts shaking Vin's shoulders, I pull her away.

"Don't do that. He could have a concussion!"

"Is he alive?" Nova looks at me, her face deathly pale. "Please tell me he's alive!"

I bend over Vin. His face looks so peaceful that for a moment I fear the worst.

But then I feel his warm breath on my hand.

"He's breathing! We need to take him inside."

I try not to look at the blood on Vin's forehead as I struggle to turn him onto his back. Then I slide my hands under his armpits. As I drag him to the front door, his heels leave a trail in the gravel. Vin groans and his eyes open. "Wh-what's going on?"

"Vin." Nova takes hold of his hand and presses it to her lips. "Everything's going to be okay. We're here."

With difficulty, I get Vin through the front door. Nova and I lift him onto the couch.

Vin feels the wound on his forehead. "I was outside. I . . ."

"Shhh, don't talk." Nova points at the first-aid kit, which is still on the coffee table. "Shouldn't we disinfect it?"

"Yes . . . yes, of course." I act quickly, pressing some gauze to Vin's skin and sticking it down with two Band-Aids. Luckily, the wound soon stops bleeding. Nova and Vin have both been incredibly lucky.

"She was going to hit me on the back of the head, but Spot warned me in time." Vin is looking at Spot, who is standing beside the couch. "He growled and I turned to look. So the piece of wood hit me on the forehead."

"Did you see her?" asks Nova.

"Just a flash." Vin frowns, as if he's trying to squeeze the memory out. "I just remember her eyes. I saw pure hate. We . . . we really broke her. It's our fault that she's doing this now. I . . ."

"Take it easy." I gently push him back onto the cushions. "You probably have a mild concussion, so you need to stay calm. Maybe you should . . ."

"Take some antibiotics?" Vin says.

We all burst out laughing, but then Vin clutches his head.

"Ow, I shouldn't laugh. . . ."

"We spoke to Reid," I say. "He's coming here tomorrow morning."

"What?" The color drains from Vin's face. "How did you manage that?"

I think back to the phone call. If Vin knew the terrible things I had to say to get Reid to come here . . .

"Never mind," says Vin, turning his head away from me. "I don't want to know."

FALL

"Live music?"

The whole dance committee fell silent when I suggested my idea.

"How do you picture that?" Reid Hunter looked at me the way only he could.

Interested.

As if I mattered.

"A real orchestra," I said. "Piano, strings. That's what you need for a ball, isn't it?"

"Brilliant," said Reid Hunter.

After the meeting, he came over to me.

"Why don't you come to my place tomorrow? Then we can discuss your plans some more."

* * *

A pretty woman with shoulder-length brown hair came into the living room carrying two cups of tea.

"I'm Karen." She handed me one of the mugs, then held out her hand. "You must be Robin. Reid has told me a lot about you."

I felt my cheeks glowing and quickly took a sip of my tea.

"And all of it good," she added quickly.

I liked her right away.

"Robin has some awesome ideas for the dance," said Reid Hunter. "I think it's going to be a big success."

After school, I'd agreed to meet Reid Hunter in the music room.

There was a piece of classical music that I thought would be perfect to open the ball.

I wanted to play it for him on the piano.

But he had canceled.

A student had detention.

Again.

I walked along the school's empty halls.

Reid Hunter's classroom was on the top floor, at the very back.

The French room was next to his.

I slipped inside.

There was a window between the two rooms, but I saw that the blinds on his side had been pulled down.

What did he have to hide?

Right at the bottom, there was a small gap, just big enough for me to peep through.

I stooped to look through the crack.

Reid Hunter was sitting on one of the desks, with a girl between his legs.

It took me a second to grasp what was happening.

The girl was in a skimpy top with spaghetti straps; her hands were under his shirt.

They were moving quickly, expertly, as if they'd done this dozens of times before.

It was really true: Reid Hunter and Lotus.

She really wasn't coming to the meetings because of me, but because of him.

I took out my phone.

LOTUS

I throw an extra block of wood onto the fire. The flames lick at it as I sit back down. Slowly, the living room becomes warmer.

"It almost feels like a vacation." Nova stares into the flames.

I know what she means. When we went skiing in second grade, we sat by the fire every night. We read books and played question games to get to know each other even better. Questions we often already knew the answers to.

"Almost," I say. "If you ignore Robin and the bear traps."

Vin is snoring quietly. He fell asleep on the couch opposite, with his head on Nova's lap.

"Do you think he's still mad at me because of Reid?"

"Probably." Nova sighs. "He can be so fussy when he doesn't get his way."

"Typical only child," I say. "He always has his way at home."

"Yeah, sure does. His dad's a softie. Doesn't dare say no to him. I bet things would be different if his mom was still in the picture."

Vin lets out such a loud snore that Nova bursts out laughing.

"I can barely say no to him either, though. Let alone get mad at him. It's those damn big brown eyes of his."

"That'll be it." I look at Nova, who is gently stroking some hair out of his face.

"Why don't you tell him where you know Robin from? I'm sure he'd want to know."

Nova looks up. "No. Then things will never be the same again."

"Why not?"

"It would make him see me differently. And I don't want him to. With him, I can be the Nova I want to be. You don't want Reid Hunter to know the truth about Robin either, do you?"

I shake my head. "But . . . what Robin did in the past doesn't make *you* a worse person. It's more the opposite, I'd say. I think Vin would understand better why we hate her so much."

"Why does he need to understand?" Nova looks at me. "That's never been necessary before."

I watch the flames slowly devouring the blocks of

wood. She's kind of right: Vin always joined in with us, without knowing exactly why we were giving Robin such a hard time. All he knows is that Nova knows Robin from before and that Robin hurt her really badly. Apparently, that was enough for him. He seemed blinded by Nova. He just did whatever we did.

Suddenly I feel sorry for him. He even got a head injury without knowing exactly what this is all about.

"I'll tell him one day. Promise," says Nova. "But not now."

The next morning, the cold wakes me up. It takes me a moment to realize where I am, but then I see the stuffed bear's head looking glassily at me.

We fell asleep in front of the fire! Vin and Nova are still lying on the other couch, close together. Vin's arm is around Nova's shoulder and her fingertips are touching the floor.

The fire must have gone out ages ago—the room is freezing now. When I put my bare feet on the wooden floor, Spot stretches and yawns. I open the curtains a bit and see that it's slowly getting lighter outside. It must be really early in the morning.

"See, I can learn to get up early," I say to Spot, who enthusiastically comes toward me. "Give it a little while and I'll be able to take you out for your morning walks too."

Something buzzes. My phone.

I walk to the coffee table and flip it open. This time it's Reid, from his special number.

> I'll be there around 10.

I stare at his words. How did he convince Karen that he needed to leave home so early? Some excuse about work?

I look at Vin and Nova, who are still fast asleep. A pang of jealousy hits me when I see them lying there on the couch like that. They can just be together, even fall asleep in each other's arms.

Do they have any idea how lucky that makes them?

I grab my coat and put Spot on a leash. When we get outside, he drags me to the edge of the forest and pees on a tree.

Is Robin already awake? I spin around, but there's no sign of anyone. The forest is quieter than ever—all I can hear is my own breathing.

I should go straight back inside, but I don't feel like spending any more time looking at Nova and Vin. Besides, I can always think better outside. Maybe I can come up with some ideas for later. When Reid gets here, we'll need to have a rock-solid plan or he'll turn tail and head back home with his tires screeching.

Spot and I walk part of the way toward the surfaced road, in the opposite direction from the bear traps. The forest still seems to be resting. I have the world to myself. Slowly, my heartbeat calms. I take out my phone and send a message back to Reid.

See you soon.

I consider adding my usual X, but then just end the message with a period.

Then I open the conversation with Robin. Her last message was from yesterday. Her silence is almost scarier than her threatening text messages.

What's next.

Yesterday she attacked Vin, but what happens now?

Out of habit, I call the number. I know she won't answer. After all, she has us exactly where she wants us. She's the one who decides when we have contact, not us.

But then I hear it.

From somewhere to my left, far off among the trees, a phone quietly ringing.

LOTUS

I stare in the direction of the sound. The phone only rang twice, but I clearly heard it. She's here!

For the first time, Robin has made a mistake.

I look back toward the farmhouse, which is around the corner of the track. If I go fetch Nova and Vin, she'll be long gone—I'm sure of that.

For the first time, I have an advantage and I need to use it. I wrap Spot's leash more tightly around my hand and step off the track. My heart pounding, I head toward the place the sound came from.

What am I going to find there? What will I do if Robin tries to knock me down, like she did with Vin?

But as Spot pulls me onward, my doubts give way to adrenaline. Branches lash my face, but I hardly feel them.

I step carefully over the bear traps and make Spot jump over them. I press Robin's number again, but this time there's silence. I look around, listening for the slightest sound. Ragged breathing, a twig snapping. I want to hear everything.

Then there's a cracking sound nearby, followed by footsteps.

Without thinking, I start running. Spot is barely able to keep up as I jump over roots and fallen branches. There's something white among the trees up ahead. What is it? I push some low-hanging branches out of the way and come out onto a different track.

A white RV is parked on the border. It has two red stripes down the side and Virginia plates.

I look back. How far are we from the farmhouse?

Less than three hundred yards. The thought that she's been so close to us all this time makes my head spin.

But then I see that the door is slightly open.

Is this another kind of trap? What if she actually wants me to go in there?

A little voice inside my head tells me to fetch the others. It'll be much safer with three of us.

But I need to know what her hiding place looks like. I have to find out what else she's planning.

With my foot, I push the door open. It's pretty dark inside the camper, blackout curtains covering the windows. I reach for a light switch and find one around the corner.

When I press the button, the space is filled with white light. There's no sign of anyone. The comforter is half off the bed, and there are papers on the floor. On the small gas stove, there's a pan with burned remains of pasta sauce. Empty toffee wrappers on the table, her favorite kind. This camper is definitely hers.

Spot sniffs at a cupboard, and I pick up the sheets of paper. I have to be quick—she could be back any minute.

I put the sheets of paper on the table and turn them over. I was expecting notes, a schedule for her next plan, but not this. . . .

They are all photographs.

Pictures of Reid and me.

A bit blurred, but clear enough to recognize both of us.

Reid's chin on my naked shoulder, his eyes closed. My hands under his shirt, his hands on the clasp of my bra.

How is this possible?

In my head, Reid and I were always something beautiful, but in these photographs, we look like two wild animals that can't control themselves.

WINTER

"Robin."

Suddenly they were there, in front of the supermarket: Bittersweet, Lotus, and the boy.

I'd just come out with my groceries.

"What do you want?" I hated the way my voice was shaking.

"Didn't I already tell you that?" Bittersweet peered at the contents of my cart and gave a contemptuous sniff.

I thought about the photographs I'd printed at home.

They were even better in a large format.

"I'm not leaving the school," I said. "And I'm not resigning from the dance committee either, if that's what you guys are after. Reid needs my help."

Lotus looked at me. "Reid feels sorry for you."

I clamped my hands around the handle of the cart.

Don't react.

Her time would come.

And then she'd regret everything.

"How about we take these for you?" Bittersweet grabbed a bag of toffees, a packet of cookies, and even the burgers for tonight from my cart.

I wanted to stop her, but she gave me such a glare that it felt like she'd kicked me in the stomach.

"Look at it this way—we're doing it to help you."

There was a silence.

In a flash, I remembered something.

It was something about those cold, gray eyes, something in the words she said.

Where did I know Bittersweet from?

"Robin, it's Reid."

He acted like it was the most ordinary thing in the world for him to call me, but we'd never spoken on the weekend before.

"Reid Hunter?"

Reid laughed. "Yep, that's my name. But, hey, you can call me Reid."

"Did you have a question about the dance?"

"No, I just wanted to ask if you'd like to come out sailing. Karen and I have made a picnic and we thought it would be nice if you came along. You'll need to wear warm clothes, because it's cold out on the water."

Reid feels sorry for you.

Lotus's statement echoed inside my mind.

"Say yes. It's such wonderful winter weather." Reid Hunter didn't wait for my answer. "We'll come fetch you in about half an hour."

"Isn't this beautiful?" Reid Hunter said, looking out over the water. "It's normally covered with duckweed, but in the fall . . ."

Karen gave a sigh and smiled. "Here we go again . . . Now we're going to get all the facts, Robin. When you're tired of them, just throw him overboard."

"In the fall, the duckweed sinks to the bottom for the winter. It doesn't come back up until the spring," I said, completing his sentence for him.

"Ha!" Reid Hunter grinned as he looked at his wife. "Too bad for you that Robin's just as much of a plant nerd as I am."

"Oh no . . ." Karen clutched her head. "What have I gotten myself into?"

But it didn't sound like she really minded at all.

LOTUS

"Where were you?" Vin comes storming out of the farm-house. The dressing on his forehead is now dangling from just one Band-Aid. The wound has dried up and the skin around it is yellow from the disinfectant.

"Well?"

The words stick in my throat. I can't even remember how I got back to the house.

"What do you have there?" Vin points at the sheets of paper in my hand.

I follow his gaze and realize that I'm still holding them. Startled, I drop them, as if they're on fire. The photos tumble to the ground, some with the image facing up.

"Shit . . ." Vin turns pale. "Where did you get those from?"

"She . . . she has a camper." I turn around. "She's parked just on the other side of the bear traps."

Vin's eyes grow wide. "Did you go in there on your own?"

"I had Spot with me," I say weakly.

"Spot?!" Vin points at his forehead. "Do you want to end up like this?"

"Sorry," I mumble.

"What's going on?" Nova is standing sleepily in the doorway. Shivering, she wraps her arms around herself. "Why are you guys talking so loud?"

"You stay here with Nova." Vin jabs his finger at me. "I'm going to take a look."

"Nothing." Vin comes in, his face bright red. "Robin's cleared off. All I found were a few tire tracks. I bet she's miles away by now. You should have come and got us. Then we could have done something. But no, you wanted to solve everything on your own."

Doesn't he get that I was so shocked by the phone ringing that I wasn't thinking clearly?

"Well, you just ran off there on your own too," I said.

Vin gives me a withering look but collapses onto the couch without saying anything.

"Hey, cool it, you two," says Nova. "In a couple of hours, Reid will be at the door. We need a plan. When he sees my foot and your forehead, he'll know there's something else going on."

"What do you suggest?"

"These are here in case we need them." Nova sweeps the photographs together, which are facedown on the table. She'd turned one over and immediately put it back. I'm glad she didn't say anything about them, because I feel so incredibly dirty. It's like someone made a porno of me. Those photos look so cheap.

"If Reid is difficult, you can always confront him with those."

Shocked, I look at Nova. "Is that what you want me to do?"

"If it's absolutely necessary," Nova says. "But only then."

"Reid is here." My stomach turns into a buzzing wasps' nest. He's ten minutes early, just like at school.

"You can do it," says Nova, letting go of my hand.

The plan is clear: Nova and Vin are staying upstairs. I'm going to talk to Reid on my own.

My legs are shaking as I go downstairs. When I get to the bottom step, I see a silhouette through the glass. The doorbell rings.

Just another moment and I'll see him again. Reid, the man I spent every spare minute with, the man I took huge risks for.

But now my stomach flips, as if our final exams have already begun.

I can still go back.

I can turn around, head back upstairs, and ask Nova to send him away.

But then it will all have been for nothing. We can't go back; we can only keep on going.

What's next?

I take a deep breath and open the door. Reid is standing there. As always in a shirt, done up to the top button. Tailored pants with his scuffed-up sneakers below in stark contrast with the rest.

"Lotus." His voice sounds cool and distant, as if I'm a problem student who constantly talks in his lessons. "Why are you doing this?"

Yeah, he's not going to throw his arms around me. After all, I threatened to tell his wife. He's furious.

"I have to . . ."

"Why?" Reid asks again. "Karen has nothing to do with this."

I open the door wider.

"Why don't you come in?"

"Where are Nova and Vin?"

"They've gone for a walk so that we can talk." I've practiced the lie in my head, and fortunately, it sounds convincing.

Reid follows me to the living room. Spot gives him a warm welcome, but Reid ignores him. He paces back and forth across the room.

"Would you like a cup of tea?"

"Lotus . . ." Reid stops pacing. "How much do they know?"

"Everything." *More than I wanted. They've even seen us—in black and white.*

My gaze flashes to the photographs, which are folded up on the kitchen table.

I turn my back on Reid and pour two teas. Reid picks one up—our hands touch.

"Did you . . ." Reid seems to be searching for the right words. "Did you already contact Karen?"

"Not yet."

Reid makes a small sound, somewhere between a groan and a sigh.

"Please don't. Please, Lo." Reid puts his cup on the coffee table and pulls me down onto the couch. He is sitting so close to me that I can smell his aftershave. A slightly sweet scent that smells young but mature at the same time.

"I came all the way here. Can't you at least look at me?"

I don't want to, but my eyes are drawn automatically to his. Serious, dark eyes. The eyes that always knew where to find me in class.

A few weeks ago, everyone stormed out of the room

when class was finally over. At the door, Reid pulled me back for a kiss. When I asked him why, he said he'd been thinking about it all lesson.

"Hey," Reid says cautiously. His eyes are very different now; he's a bit on his guard, like I'm a bomb that could go off at any moment. "I'm here, okay? I know that it's hard for you. But what about me? I've been lying to my wife for months now, and I'm not doing it for fun. You've made things so difficult for me and . . ."

I look up. "What?"

"Sorry, I don't mean it like that. I know it's me who's the jerk here. I just liked you so much, and the thought that you wanted to be with me . . . Well, shoot." Reid looks at me. "Are you laughing at me?"

I didn't even notice I have a smile on my lips.

"*Shoot?*" I repeat.

A twinkle appears in Reid's eyes. "What's wrong with saying *shoot?*"

"Nothing," I say, "if you're a senior citizen."

"Hey, you, watch it!" Reid gives me a challenging look. For a moment I think he's going to kiss me, but then he stands up.

"This is exactly what I mean! You and me . . . That message of yours—you were right. This has to stop."

I think about Nova and Vin sleeping in each other's arms on this couch last night.

There is no one else here. No school principal, none of

Reid's coworkers, no students, no Karen. I could just curl up next to him now and lie here with him.

"We could—" I begin, but Reid interrupts me.

"And about Karen . . ."

That name again—I'm right back to reality. Karen might not actually be here, but she's always inside his head.

"You can't tell her anything, okay? Not now."

I look at him. "What do you mean, *not now?*"

"Because . . ." Reid tugs at his curls, as if he's trying to pull the answer out of them. "Because I'm going to be a father soon."

WINTER

I was sitting across from Karen at the kitchen table.

She'd started inviting me around, even when Reid wasn't home.

"I've stopped taking the Pill."

"S-sorry?" I spluttered on the tea she'd just poured for me.

Karen smiled. "I get that it might seem a bit strange, me telling you that, but I like you, Robin. And . . . you know Reid. How do you think he'll feel about it?"

I pictured him with Lotus between his legs.

Maybe he was even with her right now.

"Um, good?"

"Yeah?" For the first time, Karen sounded a little uncertain. "I do know I need to tell him about the Pill. But talking about serious things isn't our strong suit."

Oh help.

She wanted to have his baby—and he was screwing a student.

"Looks like you'll need to have that chat" was all I said.

"Robin?"

After the next dance committee meeting, Reid stopped me.

"I just wanted to thank you."

"What for?"

"Karen talked to me. She said you'd encouraged her to be honest."

I shrugged.

"Honesty is always the best policy. Right?"

I looked at the top button of his shirt and left a short silence.

"No matter how painful the truth is."

"Robin!" Reid came cycling into my street.

I put the key in the lock and pretended not to hear him.

"Robin!" He braked right beside me. "Are your mom and dad home?"

"No."

"Could I just talk to you for a moment?"

I saw the despair in his eyes.

He knew that I knew.

"Please."

He had helped me on the first day.

Thanks to him, I'd felt—just for a moment—that everything was going to be okay.

"All right."

We went and sat opposite each other in the living room.

"I know I'm screwing up." Reid just blurted it out, like Karen did with the Pill. "But I love my wife."

"Then why are you doing this? Karen is worth her weight in gold!"

"I know Karen is amazing but . . ."

"You just want to have sex with Lotus."

Reid looked at me, shocked. "Yes. Yes, something like that."

"You have to stop," I said. "It's wrong. And you're going to be a father!"

"You're right." Reid nodded. "I'll put a stop to it."

LOTUS

"You're going to be a father?" It's as if all the oxygen has been sucked out of the room.

"Karen's pregnant." Reid lets his arms hang beside his body. "I'm sorry."

"What for?"

"For everything, Lo." Reid walks back to the couch and sits down beside me again. "Believe me, I didn't want it to—"

I slap him right in the face. There's a bright-red mark on his cheek.

Reid hangs his head and mumbles something.

"What?" I snap at him.

"I deserved that." Reid looks at me. His eyes are sad and sorry, and for a moment he looks just like Robin, who was also good at that expression. Like everything always just kind of happened to her, like she wasn't to blame for anything.

"Do you know why you're really here?" Inside my head, I tear up our script. I'm going to tear open all the wounds at once. I want to hit Reid where it hurts. "Because Robin's here."

Reid gives me a puzzled frown.

"Robin is here. You told her where we were staying— and she followed us here."

Reid's face is one big question mark.

"She knows about the two of us, Reid. She's been threatening me because of our affair. She's sending me messages, on my secret phone."

I take out the old-fashioned cell phone. "Did you give her this number?"

"N-no . . . ," stammers Reid. "No, why would I?"

"Because you wanted to get rid of me?"

"You wanted to get rid of *me*," says Reid. "You sent that message that you wanted to stop."

"And that suited you just fine, didn't it?"

Reid blushes deep red.

"So you could start a nice little family with that Karen of yours." I feel sick. That woman doesn't know anything about this, and there's a baby growing inside her. The ultimate proof of their love.

And there was me thinking that I mattered to him.

I get up and go stand by the big sliding door. "Robin is going to kill me."

"I don't get it." Reid comes and stands behind me. "Why would she do something like that?"

How does he still not get it? Even after I gave him a slap, he still seems half asleep.

"When she came to you with that story about us bullying her, it wasn't a lie. It was true."

Now that I've started, the truth comes pouring out. None of it matters anymore.

"We made her life hell all those months, and now she's doing the same to us. She left the school because of us."

Silence.

"She took photos, Reid. From the French room, when we . . . You hadn't pulled the blinds down far enough."

More silence.

"There's photographic evidence. Do you understand? It doesn't matter anymore if I keep my mouth shut. This is going to come out anyway."

I finally turn around. Reid's face is so pale that it's almost transparent, and a muscle in his temple is twitching.

"There are . . . photos?"

Has he got it at last?

"Yes. Lots of them."

"But . . ." Reid shakes his head. "She'd never do something like that to me. I'm her friend. You guys . . . you must have broken her. What did you do to her?"

"That doesn't matter."

"Of course it does." Reid grabs me by my shirt. It happens so suddenly that it scares me speechless. One moment he's standing there, defeated; the next, his face is so close to mine that I can hardly focus on it.

"TELL ME!"

Upstairs, there's creaking, followed by rapid footsteps down the stairs. A moment later, Vin comes into the living room, followed by a limping Nova.

"Hey!" Vin yells.

Startled, Reid lets go of my shirt as Vin takes a threatening step in his direction.

"Move away from Lotus." Vin's voice is even hoarser than usual. "Now!"

Reid takes a step back with his hands in the air, as if Vin is holding him at gunpoint.

"You okay?" Nova asks me.

I nod, but my throat feels thick and painful, as if that was where Reid had grabbed me.

"What is all this?" Reid looks at Vin's head wound and then at Nova's taped-up foot. "What happened to you guys?"

"Oh, this?" Nova points at her bandage. "That's thanks to Robin. You know, your charming coworker."

He shouldn't be here.
I've always liked that guy, but now he's getting in the way.

LOTUS

Reid is staring at Nova as if she just slapped him too. I know how he feels now. He's trying to grasp everything that's going on.

Robin, his favorite coworker.

Reid took her under his wing right from day one, probably because the principal had asked him to.

But why did he continue to spend time with her? Why did he ask her to join the dance committee? It had to be pity, right?

I wanted him to see her as we saw her. Robin had no business being at our school—it was Nova's domain. When she came to work at Oakwood High, it felt like she was giving Nova an extra kick. The stupid bitch didn't even recognize Nova!

"Th-that's impossible," says Reid. "Robin couldn't have done this."

Even now he's sticking up for her. I can feel my hands tingling.

"We have the proof on my phone," I say.

"I don't understand, Lotus." Reid looks at me. "Why did you make me come here? What do I have to do with all this?"

Nova lets out a little laugh. "Are you serious? Everything started with you! You were the one who had to start something with a student!"

"Lotus seduced me. I just got carried away."

"It doesn't matter who seduced who—you're a teacher, an adult. She's your student. You should be in jail." Nova spits out the words. "Pathetic jerk."

"Sorry?"

"I said you're a pathetic jerk."

I feel my cheeks becoming warm. Nova was furious when she found out about Reid, but now she's totally on my side.

"So, what's it going to be?" Nova puts her hands on her hips. "Are you going to help us to stop Robin, or not?"

He doesn't say anything.

"There are photographs. Did Lotus tell you that already?"

"You guys are not going to blackmail me," Reid whispers.

"*Us?*" Nova laughs. "What about Robin? She's the one who took the photos of you. Not us!"

"No." Reid shakes his head frantically. "No, no, no. I am not going to listen to this. I'm going."

He walks out.

At first no one reacts, but then Vin starts moving. Nova holds him back.

"Let me go. I'll punch that guy's lights out if I have to. What an incredible . . ."

"No," Nova says. "Lotus has to do it."

When I look up, I see Nova staring at me. "Go on."

"Yeah . . ." I run outside, where Reid has already gotten into his car. As he starts the engine, I pull open the passenger door and sit down beside him.

"Lotus . . ." Reid sounds threatening. "Get out of my car. Now."

"No." I pull the safety belt around me and fasten it. "If you're going back home, I'm going with you."

"Lotus!"

"No," I say again.

Reid slams the steering wheel. "Shit!"

At least it's better than shoot.

"What do you want from me?" Reid hits the steering wheel again. "I'm going to lose everything. Everything! My career, my wife, my child, my freedom. I'll get sent to jail. I . . ." Reid starts crying. He slumps on the steering wheel and the horn goes off.

I lean forward and take the key from the ignition. The engine stops—and suddenly there's absolute silence.

I stare numbly at the farmhouse.

Why did I ask Reid to come here? He's not going to help us. All he cares about is himself. *His* career, *his* wife, *his* unborn child, and *his* freedom. It doesn't matter what happens to me. Maybe I never meant anything to him at all.

"Just go."

Reid finally looks up, his eyes bloodshot.

"W-what?"

"Just go home." I undo my seat belt and throw the key into his lap. It's as if I just woke up after sleeping for months.

"Go home to your wife. We'll deal with this by ourselves."

"Lotus?" Nova comes into the hallway. She doesn't ask me any questions, just puts her arms around me. She strokes my hair. I try not to cry.

How could Reid be so selfish? How does he dare to say this has nothing to do with him?

The threats started because of what happened between us!

"I'm sorry." Nova presses a kiss on my cheek. "He really is a jerk."

Then there are three knocks on the front door. Nova

yanks open the door and just about spits out the words: "What do you want?"

"I . . ." Reid is having a hard time getting the words out. "You were right."

Nova stands like a bodyguard in front of me. "What do you mean?"

"I seduced Lotus, not the other way around. I am a pathetic jerk, who cheated on his wife and abused his position. Now let me help you guys."

There is a silence. Nova looks over her shoulder at me. "What are we going to do?"

I see that Reid's eyes are still red. All I really want to do is slam the door in his face, but we need him.

"Let him come in."

WINTER

"How about looking here for a dress?" Karen had linked arms with me and was pulling me toward a clothes store. "I think they'll have something nice for the dance."

Moments later, Karen held up a dress. "This one?"

It was perfect, exactly what I had in mind.

"Beautiful."

I looked at Karen's happy face.

"Why are you doing this?"

"What?"

"Why are you helping me?"

Karen looked puzzled. "Because we're friends, of course."

I was bubbling away inside.

I hadn't had any girlfriends since elementary school.

The bullying started when I was about twelve and after that I had erected a high wall and let hardly anyone in.

"Aren't we?" Karen said when I didn't respond.

"Yes, of course," I said quickly.

"Go on, then." She pushed me toward the fitting room. "Try it on!"

"It's perfect on you." My mom looked at me in the mirror. "That friend of yours made a good call."

That friend of yours.

I tasted the words on my tongue.

They were even better than toffees.

"Hey, why is it that you still live with your parents?" asked Bittersweet after the lesson. Lotus and the boy were standing by the door. "Can't cut the ties with Mommy and Daddy?"

I picked up my stuff.

If I ignored them, they'd give up eventually.

That was what I'd learned at teacher training.

But as advice to give to students.

Was I seriously expected to follow it myself?

"It's a good thing you don't have a boyfriend." Bittersweet was not going to stop. "He'd run off screaming if he saw your little pink princess bedroom."

I swung around.

What did she know about me?

"What?" Bittersweet smiled, like she always did. "You going to hit me or something?"

There was nothing I would have liked more, but I knew I had to wait.

Her turn would come.

My trump card would be legendary.

LOTUS

"What are we doing here?" asks Vin. "That RV is long gone!"

Reid kneels down. "There are still tracks. And these ones are fresh."

"Biology teacher and Boy Scout in one." Nova sniffs. "We're so lucky to have you."

Reid ignores her comment and stands up. "If we follow this track, we'll know where she is."

My eyes follow the weaving tire tracks, which go deeper into the forest.

"She could be miles away," I say. "That's never going to work with Nova's foot."

"Then Nova and Vin can wait back at the house," says Reid.

I look at her. Nova seems to understand that I don't want to be alone with Reid and shakes her head.

"Vin and Lotus can go together."

"What about me?" asks Reid.

"You're coming to the house with me. We need to keep you back until the right moment," says Nova, like Reid is some kind of surprise act. "Okay?"

She directs that last question mainly at me, and I nod gratefully.

"Let's go." Reid gives Vin and me a stern look. Suddenly he seems like the teacher he is at school again. "If you guys find the camper, then call me. There have been enough injuries, so don't do anything by yourselves. Got it?"

"Poor Reid," says Vin as we follow the tracks. "Nova is going to tear him apart."

"That's his own fault," I say, just a little too loudly.

Vin gives me a sideways glance. "Are you really completely done with him?"

"Like you were suddenly done with Nova?"

I see Vin's shoulders tense up. "Are we seriously going to talk about that now?"

"Better than in the middle of the night, with Nova asleep five yards away."

Vin looks at me. "Why are you being like this?"

"You've been making me lie to Nova for weeks," I say. "And I don't want to."

"And I've been trying to talk to you for weeks," Vin says defensively.

"But I didn't want to hear it before now."

Maybe it's because of the conversation with Reid, which finally made me realize that I'm in the same boat as Vin. Only I'm not the one who's cheating on someone. But Reid did cheat on his wife with me. Does that make me any less guilty?

Vin takes a deep breath. "You should never have seen it."

I think back to a few weeks ago, when I took Spot for a quick walk in the neighborhood. It was raining, so I skipped the woods.

And suddenly I saw Vin. It was already dark, but I recognized him immediately by the way he walks. Vin always walks so slowly, like he needs to think about every step.

I was about to call his name, but then I saw he wasn't alone.

He was with a girl.

His hand was entwined with hers.

And that girl was not Nova.

Maybe I should have turned around, but instead I walked a few yards behind them.

Vin stopped under a lamppost. He slid his hand into the girl's hair and leaned in. They kissed, for minutes. They were so absorbed in each other that the rain didn't seem to touch them.

Frozen, I stood there watching, until Spot whimpered in protest.

I took a side road and headed home. All the way there, my heart was pounding and even in bed I couldn't get my breathing under control.

"Do you know I thought at first that I'd gotten it wrong? That it actually *was* Nova? I couldn't believe you'd do something like that."

The track splits and we take the path on the right.

"I thought the same about you," says Vin. "I never would have thought you and Reid . . ."

"But why don't you just break up with Nova?"

"Because then I'd lose *this*." Vin points at me and then at himself. "I want the three of us to stay together."

For a moment, I fall silent.

"But you're in love with someone else!"

Vin shakes his head. "Stella was a mistake. I love Nova. But sometimes . . . sometimes she seems like a very different Nova than she was when I met her. And then I'm kind of scared of her."

I picture the way Nova looks whenever the subject of Robin comes up. It's like a switch flicks and she changes into a completely different person.

"Nova doesn't deserve this," I say. "You have to be honest with her. Like I told you right away."

Vin laughs nervously. "I nearly had a heart attack when I saw your message."

I nod. "You realized you'd been caught."

"No." Vin looks at me. "I knew you'd take Nova's side. That you always will."

"I've known Nova almost my entire life," I say, defending myself.

"Exactly, I can never compete with that." Vin walks on. "Can I?"

"You have to talk to Nova" is my only answer. "Not to me."

We continue along the track. How much farther do we have to go? I'm about to give up when Vin suddenly stops.

"Is that the camper?"

Among the leaves along the track, I can see a big white vehicle with red stripes on the side. That's it!

I pull Vin into the trees and we creep closer. I take my phone out of my pocket.

"What are you doing?" whispers Vin.

"Calling Reid. That was the deal." I look at the signal. One bar—is that enough?

It seems to take an eternity, but then the phone finally rings. Blood thumps in my ears when someone answers.

"Reid?" I can barely control my voice. "You're right. They were fresh tracks. The camper is here. We're about half a mile from the spot where we split up. You have to go right at the fork."

There's silence on the other end of the line.

"Will you bring Nova here? Maybe you can carry her part of the way. Vin and I will wait here."

Why isn't he saying anything?

I look at the screen again. Have I lost my signal?

But when I put the phone back to my ear, I hear a woman's voice.

"Lotus?" The way Robin says my name makes my body freeze. "I suggest you guys come to the house instead."

And then the line goes dead.

WINTER

"Did you always want to be a teacher?"

We were sitting in Karen's favorite café.

"No, I had another job before this."

"Can I be honest with you?" Karen didn't wait to hear my answer. "I think you look deeply unhappy."

"Oh" was all I said.

"Are the students giving you a hard time?" Karen looked at me so kindly that I almost started crying. "I know how that feels. Seriously. Sometimes you just want to murder them."

I was certain she had no idea of what the students were doing to me—and what I was letting them get away with.

Karen was Karen, a woman who was always the center of attention without even trying.

She was probably just as popular as Reid.

"Yes," I said. "Sometimes you want to kill them."

* * *

"Just a few more days until the dance!" Reid said, ending the last meeting.

"And I have a question for Robin—would you like to open the event? After all, the masked ball was your idea."

Give a speech to the whole school?

Never.

But Reid was like his wife—he never waited for the answer.

"Great." He clapped his hands. "We're all set."

"You're going to give a speech before the dance?"

The three of them hung around after class.

"You really think anyone wants to listen to you?"

LOTUS

Robin is with . . . That's all I can think about as I sprint toward the house.

"Lotus!" Vin's voice sounds very far away.

What if I'm too late?

Has she already hurt Nova?

I never should have left her behind on her own. Seems not even Reid could protect her.

"Lotus!"

There were the two of us, following tire tracks, chasing her down, like a couple of scouts. Meanwhile, Robin had all the time she needed to overpower Nova.

I see Nova's foot again, covered in blood. Maybe this time it'll be even worse. What if Robin is armed?

I push branches out of the way and see the red tiles of the farmhouse.

Please, let me be in time.

I shove my shoulder against the door and burst into the house. I run through the hall, across the wooden boards to the living room. When I throw open that door, too, I see Nova sitting on the couch with her foot on the coffee table. Spot is lying on her other foot, with the big bone I brought from home.

"Lotus?"

My eyes dart around the room, looking for Robin. Where is she?

"Hey, you're back." Reid looks up from the kitchen table. "You guys were going to call me, weren't you?"

What's going on? Why is no one panicking?

"Where . . . where is she?"

"Who?" Nova sits up.

"Robin." Vin stands panting behind me. "Where is she?!"

Reid frowns. "What are you guys talking about?"

"She answered your phone," I yell. "She said we should come here. I thought she was with you. I thought she . . ."

I don't even dare to finish the sentence.

"How can she have my phone?" Reid takes his phone from his pocket. "Are you sure it was Robin? Not my voice mail?"

What a dumb question. I'd recognize her voice anywhere.

But then I see which phone Reid is holding up.

"We called your other number. *Our* phone."

Reid looks pale. "That one's still in the car. . . ."

He jumps up and runs to the front door. I hear the gravel crunch under his shoes and then there's a curse from outside.

When Reid comes back inside, his face is as gray as Vin's. "I didn't lock my door. The other phone's gone."

Spot has finally stopped chewing and has fallen asleep on the last scrap of bone.

I look at Reid, who is sitting on the couch opposite me, looking deathly pale. He seems to have gotten older, as if the past few hours weren't hours but years. He's twisting the gold wedding ring on his finger.

He never wore his ring when we were together. He always used to leave the thing in his desk drawer.

My phone buzzes. The sound comes as such a shock that we all jump to our feet.

I'm the first to reach the phone, which is on the coffee table. Vin, Nova, and Reid lean forward to read the message with me. When I open the flap, I see that the message is from Reid's secret phone.

> It's so good that you're all together.
> Welcome, Reid.

"Is that all?" asks Nova in surprise, but then another message arrives.

> Too bad you deleted so much of your history, but the last few messages are enough. Does Karen already know that you think Lotus is a better kisser than her?

Reid curses under his breath. I hardly dare to look at him. I remember that message word for word. He sent it less than a week ago, just before I went to sleep. His messages usually came in the evening, because Karen always goes to bed before him.

It was those rare moments when we could talk without worrying about being disturbed. Sometimes we sent each other dozens of messages before we finally went to sleep.

> But do you know what that "best kisser" did at the school dance? Maybe you should have a good conversation about that night. And NO LIES. Teachers have eyes and ears everywhere.

I feel my stomach flip. I knew Robin would bring it up. "What does she mean?" asks Reid. It takes me a moment to realize he's talking to me. "Lotus?"

I see myself again in that purple dress. Warner laughed at me, but Mom thought I looked amazing. I walked to school, because there was no way I could ride a bike with that big skirt.

I didn't want to admit it, but Robin's idea for a masked ball was actually kind of cool. When I got to school and saw Vin and Nova there, it felt like going back in time. Vin was wearing a beautiful suede suit with a bow tie; Nova was in a flouncy dress like me, but hers was jet black. And she wasn't wearing her usual shoes, but pretty little slippers.

"What's Robin talking about?" Reid insists. "What happened at the dance?"

One chance to tell the truth.

Is she going to lie again to save her own skin?

Or is she finally willing to show her true self?

WINTER

As soon as the school came into view, the nerves really started.

Within a few minutes, I'd be giving a speech to the whole school.

"Don't worry about it," Dad said as he pulled up to the building. "You're going to have a great night."

I thought about Reid.

If I stayed close to him, they couldn't do anything to me.

Even Karen was going to be there.

She didn't want to miss a moment of my big night.

"I'll pick you up here," said Dad, giving me a wink. "Don't forget to have fun, eh?"

"Hey, you're here!" Reid greeted me with as much enthusiasm as on my first day.

He was wearing a brown suit, which looked perfect with his eyes.

He'd even swapped his scuffed-up sneakers for new ones.

The orchestra we'd booked played beautifully, but I couldn't enjoy it.

The thought that I'd soon be standing up in front of the entire school and . . .

"You ready?" Reid said, pushing the curtain aside.

All I could see was a bright spotlight. The orchestra stopped playing.

My footsteps sounded heavy and clumsy on the wooden stage.

At the front of the stage, a microphone was waiting for me. I wrapped my trembling hands around the stand.

Slowly, my eyes got used to the bright lights and I saw the outlines of the students.

Their voices fell silent.

I heard someone cough.

Was it Reid?

I took a deep breath.

"Welcome, everyone. Welcome to the ball."

The faces on the front row looked at me expectantly.

But then I saw Bittersweet, standing right at the side.

Beside her were Lotus and the boy.

All three took their masks out at the same moment and put them on.

They were pig masks.

LOTUS

"What?" Reid looked at me with a frown.

Do I really need to repeat that?

"Pig masks."

"But . . . I saw you that evening. You were wearing a normal mask."

"Not when she gave her speech."

Reid shakes his head. "Why on earth . . . ?"

"Because we wanted to throw her off balance. We wanted her to fail up there onstage."

"Well, you succeeded. It was an embarrassing display. She just stood there, floundering." Reid makes a face, as if the memory is physically painful. "And why pig masks? Because she's a bit . . . on the heavy side?"

"On the heavy side?" Nova spits the words out.

Reid looks shocked. "Hey . . ."

"It's the truth, isn't it?"

"And what's wrong with that?" Reid looks at Nova, then me, and back again. "Was that seriously the reason you guys bullied her out of the school? Because she was fat? What kind of crap is that?"

"You have no idea," I say quietly.

"No. I don't." Reid points at the phone. "Seems Robin has every right to treat you like this."

Nova stands up. "Take that back."

"Or what? You guys going to bully me too?"

"Robin is not a victim," I say.

"Really? If I'm not mistaken, you guys drove her crazy for months and just when she was at her weakest, on that big stage, you put on pig masks to embarrass her even more!"

"Robin is *not* a victim," I say again.

"Yes, she is!" Reid's voice cracks. "I should have believed her when she confided in me. *They're tearing me to shreds*—those were her exact words. I thought she was exaggerating. I couldn't believe you would ever do something like that."

Reid's eyes are furious. He's looking at me as if I'm a monster.

I wish I could take back my words, because I know Reid will never forget them.

"Robin deserves it all," I say, breaking the deal I had with Nova when I say out loud: "She destroyed my best friend."

"Lotus . . ." Nova looks at me in horror. "No . . ."

"I have to explain," I say. "Robin doesn't get to play the victim anymore. I'm not going to let her do that."

I look at Reid and Vin.

"Robin worked at our elementary school."

My words leave such a long silence that I start to wonder if I actually said them out loud.

But then Vin looks at Nova with wide eyes. "What?"

Nova doesn't react. She hides her face in her hands.

"Nova was being bullied really badly at the time."

"Stop," says Nova between her fingers. "Please. Stop."

"They need to know." I take hold of Nova's hand, which feels small and fragile. "Nova, *you* are the victim here, not Robin!"

"What . . . did you get bullied about?" Reid asks cautiously.

Nova looks up. Her mascara has left dark circles under her eyes. "My weight."

WINTER

I had to get away from that stage.

I ran past Reid and flung open the doors to the hallway.

The teachers' restrooms were deserted. I opened a stall and sat down.

Why did I let them throw me off like that?

But as soon as I saw those masks, it felt like I was twelve again.

"Remember the photos," I mumbled to myself.

I dug my nails into my palms.

"Your moment will come."

But it didn't work.

I burst into tears.

There was a creak.

The door to the restroom was opening.

It was probably Reid coming to see how I was doing.

Or maybe he'd sent Karen.

But then I heard the grunting.

"Piggy?" Bittersweet said. "Are you in here?"

LOTUS

"You got bullied about your *weight*?" Vin looks at Nova in disbelief.

"When I was little, I was fat." Nova stares ahead, as if she is seeing herself as she was then. I remember our class photo, with Nova and me sitting at the front. I was in a dress, Nova in a baggy T-shirt. The bullying was at a peak then. Nova sometimes called in sick because she was too scared to come to school.

There was that time at her house when she took a pair of scissors to the class photograph. She kept scratching away at her face until she was no longer visible.

"But . . ." Vin looks at Nova. "What did they do?"

"They made grunting sounds when I walked past, they stuck pictures of pigs in my planner, they said I smelled like bacon." Nova lists the facts as if it's a shopping list.

"And one afternoon they were waiting for me after school. They put tape on my nose and . . ."

I feel my stomach clench at the memory, as if it had happened to me.

"They pulled my nose up and stuck it there. It was that super-strong construction tape. I couldn't get it off."

I remember Nova coming to my house, with her scarf over her face. I'd had to go to the dentist that day, so I'd left school early. She said she needed my help and made me promise not to laugh.

When my friend lowered the scarf, I saw what they'd done. Nova shouldn't have worried about me laughing at her. It was such a disgusting thing to do that it made me feel sick. As I picked the tape off her face, the tears ran down Nova's cheeks. It was the only time in elementary school that I saw her crying.

Even when those bullies eventually pushed her off the climbing frame and she cracked a bone, she didn't make a sound.

"I said she had to tell our teacher," I say, "and report the bullies."

Nova nods. "But our teacher was on maternity leave, so we had a replacement. I didn't trust that woman. Besides, the bullies would have noticed if I'd hung around to talk to the teacher after class. They were always watching me."

"So what did you do?" asks Reid.

"One day I had to go see the school doctor, like everyone in the class. When I was in her office, I blurted it out. That they called me a fat pig."

"And that school doctor was Robin," Reid concludes softly. He falls back onto the cushions with a deep sigh. "What happened?"

"She said that the other kids shouldn't call me a fat pig, but that they did have a bit of a point. That I was way too heavy and it would be great if I could lose a few pounds. That I'd brought the bullying upon myself by being so fat."

It hurts to hear Nova saying this, even though she's told me about it before. Whatever possessed Robin to say such a thing? Nova went to her for help, and Robin just sent her home with a diet. As if Nova was the problem, not the bullies.

"A few days later, she spoke to me in the hallway. She said she was doing it to help me, and she suggested that my parents should come into school for a conversation about a healthy diet. She seriously said that! With everyone else around! One of the bullies heard it all—and from that moment it got much worse."

Nova's voice is almost breaking. I look at her. She claws her hair with her hands. When we were twelve, she dyed her hair a different color. She went on an extreme diet and started dressing like Romy. As if she wanted to erase the old Nova forever. The only bit of her old life that was allowed to remain was me.

"I don't believe you."

I'm startled by Vin's harsh words.

"Sorry? You think we made it up?!"

"You must have. Why did you never tell me anything about this before?"

I feel my blood boiling. *"Sometimes it's better to keep silent.* Right?"

Vin's face clouds over, but it works. He stops talking.

"Robin told me she was a school doctor once, but it had always been her dream to teach," says Reid.

"Yeah." Nova clenches her fists. "That woman came strolling into our school. . . ."

"At first I thought she was going to give Nova more of the same treatment." I feel the fury bubbling up again. "But she didn't even *recognize* her."

"Because I'd lost weight," says Nova.

"Because Robin is a stuck-up bitch," I correct her. "You should never have taken her seriously, even though she was an adult. She was just projecting her own pain onto you!"

Nova nods slowly.

"Robin needed to leave our school, Reid. I didn't want Nova to have another relapse. She was finally eating a bit normally again!"

I look at Vin, who is standing by the glass sliding door. He's staring outside, as if his thoughts are somewhere else entirely.

Why doesn't he believe us? I want to give him a good shake—how dare he doubt our story?

"How was Nova going to get better if she was confronted with the past every day?"

"So Robin had to go," says Reid. "And how did you finally manage to make that happen?"

WINTER

Before I could lock the door, it flew open.

The three pigs' heads were looking down at me, with black holes for eyes.

"Grab her," said Bittersweet.

I felt two hands like vises around my upper arms.

"Guard the door," she snarled at the boy.

What were they going to do to me?

In this part of the school, no one could hear me scream.

The orchestra was playing, and everyone was on the dance floor.

Fear swept through my body like swarming insects.

"Don't . . ."

But Bittersweet completely ignored my plea.

"So you refuse to leave, do you?"

I tried to pull myself away, but the hands around my upper arms didn't move an inch.

Bittersweet took something from her bag, and I saw the flash of metal.

"No . . ."

She waved the scissors in front of my face.

"I'll leave. I swear it. I'll hand in my notice. I . . ."

I couldn't see it, but I knew Bittersweet was smiling under her mask.

"How did you put it again? *I'm doing this to help you.*"

That sentence again.

I could almost remember where I knew the girl from, but it was like there was a filter over my memories.

Everything seemed hazy.

"Please," I begged again. "Don't hurt me."

Bittersweet lowered the scissors, and I felt my breathing speed up.

She stroked the sharp tip over my bare skin.

She was going to stab me.

I felt something warm running down between my legs.

Was it blood?

Then I heard the sound of the scissors.

She was cutting my dress to pieces.

"Wh-why?" I stammered. "I've never done anything to hurt you!"

Suddenly those strong hands let go of me.

Lotus pulled off her mask. "Yes, you have."

"Lotus . . ." Bittersweet shook her head. "Leave her. She's not worth it. Come on. She's covered in piss."

"Someone's coming." The boy looked over his shoulder. "Quick."

Bittersweet pushed Lotus ahead of her into the hallway.

The boy hesitated, then took off his mask and looked back at me.

"Vin," they shouted. "Leave her. Come on!"

The boy was still standing there.

Was he going to help me?

"Go on," I heard myself say.

And then he left too.

LOTUS

"I don't know what to say." Reid rubs his unshaven cheeks.

"You don't need to say anything," says Nova. "That's what happened. And I don't regret any of it."

"Me neither," I say.

We look at Vin, but he's still standing with his back toward us. Why isn't he saying anything? He can't be feeling remorse, can he? I remember him lingering in the doorway to the bathroom. We were already halfway down the hall when Nova called to him.

When Reid eventually told us that Robin wouldn't be coming back, I exchanged a quick glance with Nova. We'd won. She'd finally given up.

Neither of us ever asked Vin how he felt about it. Should we have asked him? Did he feel guilty about us leaving her behind in the bathroom stall with her dress cut up and covered in urine?

Maybe I should have felt guilty, too, but all I saw was the person who'd talked Nova deeper into the abyss when she was at her most defenseless. It's because of Robin that the extreme weight loss began. Thanks to her, Nova doesn't dare to be alone. She feels too vulnerable.

Reid takes out his phone. For a moment, I wonder if he's going to report us. I have no idea how the police treat things like this, but it wouldn't end well.

But then I see his thumbs flashing over the keys. "I'm letting Robin know that you've told me the truth."

I picture Robin in her camper van, reading the message. She said she has eyes and ears everywhere, that she'll find out if we lie.

Strangely, lying never even occurred to me.

"What now?" Nova wonders out loud.

"I don't know," I say. I try to imagine what Robin's next step will be. Maybe she'll call Karen, to tell her that her husband had an affair with a student.

Would she really be capable of telling a pregnant woman something like that?

At that moment, my phone buzzes again. Here it comes—she's going to give us more orders.

You can go.

"You can go?" Nova reads out loud.

I shake my head. "Really?"

"Probably more on the way," Reid says, staring at the screen.

But nothing happens.

"This isn't right. She made that threat about our chat history. Those photos . . ."

I look at the photographs, which are still folded up on the kitchen table. Why wouldn't she take advantage of this opportunity? She has a weapon in her hands that's more powerful than a gun. She could destroy Reid and me. So, why doesn't she?

"It's a trap." Nova shakes her head. "How much do you want to bet that if we step outside, we'll be electrocuted?"

No one moves. I look at the phone in the corner of the room. What if Nova's right and Robin has put some kind of booby trap by the front door?

"We can't sit here forever." I look at Vin. "What do you think, Vin?"

Vin finally turns around. His eyes are dull. It's as if he hasn't heard anything that happened in the past few minutes. When he starts talking, his voice sounds dead and flat.

"I think we can go."

"Really?" says Nova.

"That's what she said, isn't it?" Vin points at my phone. "So, we can go."

"Finally." Nova struggles to her feet.

"But . . ." I look at Nova. "What about that trap?"

"Reid can go first."

Reid laughs nervously. "Yeah, thanks."

Nova looks at Vin. "You going to come and pack?"

But Vin has already turned around again and doesn't seem to hear her.

"Vin!"

"What?!" Vin spins to look at her. "Am I supposed to go back home with you guys now? Act nice and normal, like nothing's happened? Is that what you want?"

Nova's eyes narrow. "Well, you'd know all about that, wouldn't you? Or were you planning to tell me about Stella sometime?"

It feels like the room turns upside down. Nova *knows*?

"You've been lying to me all this time. Both of you." Nova looks at me. "I was hoping one of you would tell me, but nope."

I break out in a sweat. Why didn't she say something if she knew about it?

I think about our conversation on the way to town. She said she thought Vin was acting weird. Did she know about it then? Was she giving me a chance to confess?

"How . . . ," I say. "How did you find out?"

"Your phone."

I look at the device on the table.

"Not that prehistoric thing. Your *real* phone."

The message I sent to Vin, of course. Nova often snoops around in my messages—I already knew that. That's why I had another phone for Reid.

"But . . ."

"I'm just going to assume you both had a good reason to keep it a secret." Nova looks at Vin and then at me. "That you did it because you love me or something like that."

"We do love you," I say quickly. "So much."

"What about you?" Nova looks at Vin, who still isn't saying anything. I have no idea what he's thinking now. Why isn't he doing his best to put things right? He isn't even answering Nova's question!

"Okay, then I just really want to go home now." Nova swallows the pain as she stumbles to the door. "If we can."

"I'll give you guys a ride." Reid seems relieved that the conversation between the three of us is over. He looks at me. "At least if that's what you want."

I'm about to say no, but the alternative could be even worse. If Nova knew about Stella, Romy must know too.

They're not as wild about each other as they used to be. Those were Romy's exact words.

"Fine," I say. "We'll go with you."

* * *

I look up at the animal heads on the walls. The bear's head, still at an angle, gives me a glassy stare. If you didn't know better, you might think its eyes were actually cameras.

Teachers have eyes and ears everywhere.

A chill enters my body.

Is that what Robin meant?

"You coming?" Nova takes me by the arm. "Reid's already gone out to the car."

I look up. "Did you really let him go first?"

"Of course."

I grab the handles of my bag. My phone is back inside the front pocket. Robin hasn't sent anything else. It really seems like she's letting us go.

"Are we . . ." I hardly dare to ask the question. "Are we still friends?"

"No."

The chill in my body gets worse, but what was I expecting? I should have told Nova the truth ages ago. Why did I wait so long? Was it because of the pleading look in Vin's eyes?

But then Nova nudges me. "We're not friends now, but by the time we're back in Virginia, I'm sure I'll have come around."

Somewhere deep inside me, a little flame begins to burn. It's going to be okay. It has to be okay. We're going to study at college together.

At least if we pass the exams. For the first time since we got here, I think about the weeks ahead. We haven't studied for a second and something tells me I'll barely be able to concentrate at home either.

"I'm sorry," I say. "I should have been honest with you."

I catch myself staring at the animal heads again.

"You're right." Nova turns around. "Are you coming, then? I don't want to stay here another second."

I tear my eyes away from the animal heads and follow her outside.

Vin is already in the back seat. I open the passenger door. Spot jumps onto the mat by my feet and curls up like a doughnut.

I keep my bag on my lap because the trunk is full. I look over my shoulder. Nova's big suitcase is between her and Vin. It's like a barrier to prevent them from seeing each other.

What's it going to be like when we're back home? Vin still hasn't said a word. He's playing with his key ring and the little flashlight that's hanging from it.

"No electrocution so far." Reid turns the key to start the engine. The sound almost makes me cry with relief. I can't believe we're actually going home.

"Ready?" Reid looks at each of us in turn.

"You bet." Nova sticks her middle finger up at the farmhouse. "See you never."

Reid presses the gas and we drive off into the trees.

The soft track gives way to the surfaced road, and I flip open my phone.

Reid looks at me. "And?"

"Nothing." I don't know whether to be relieved or not. It feels like an open ending, like Robin might suddenly jump out at us.

Why did she let us go?

We drive through the village and I look at the minimart, where a clerk is taking in the sign with special offers.

When we reach the highway, the sun's setting. Not much longer and it'll be dark.

What are my mom and dad going to say when I suddenly turn up in the middle of the night? Reid had better not stop outside the front door—if they see my teacher, I'll have even more explaining to do.

I look back again. Nova and Vin are each looking out of their own window. Vin is still playing with his flashlight.

Is he ever going to talk to Nova again? Or is he simply planning to go off on his trip around the world and leave everything behind?

Maybe Nova was right. Maybe it is some kind of escape. Maybe he's so used to getting his own way that he can't stand it when people accuse him of something.

How did Nova put it, again?

His dad's a softie. Doesn't dare say no to him. I bet things would be different if his mom was still in the picture.

I look at all those keys in Vin's hands. Didn't he say he

has so many of them because he keeps going back and forth between his dad's place and his mom's?

I watch him clicking the flashlight on and off, his face illuminating and then disappearing into the shadows.

Black and white.

Two faces.

I turn my eyes from him and pull the zipper of my bag. As I take out the photographs, Reid looks at me in surprise.

"You brought those with you?"

"Did you want to leave them behind?" I hold the stack of photographs between my thumb and index finger and tear it in half. Then I repeat the movement once, twice, three times, four. It feels like I'm tearing Reid and me in two. With each rip, I feel further away from him.

We'll never be together again like we were before. From now on, he's my teacher and student adviser, and that's all.

I open the window and release the bits of paper. They fly around outside the car, hitting the windows and leaving a trail behind us.

"Robin probably still has them on her phone," Reid says. "You realize that, don't you?"

I look in the side mirror at the pieces of paper lying on the road. A truck drives over them.

"I know. We'll never be rid of her."

As soon as I say the words, I suddenly know why Robin let us go.

It doesn't matter if we're in the forest in West Virginia or at home. She has Reid's extra phone, she has the photos, she has something she can use against us, always.

That's why they stink so bad. It's fear. They know they're going to be slaughtered. They just don't know when.

ALSO THAT SUMMER

"A new job?" My mom and dad both looked up from their breakfast.

"Yes."

Much to my relief, I had gotten the job.

Biology teacher.

Far away from that other school, where the students threw chairs across the classroom.

There was even one student who had threatened me with a fake gun.

He put it to my head during class and demanded a higher grade.

"Where is it?" my mom asked.

"At Oakwood High."

My dad put down his coffee. "Seriously?"

I felt my irritation growing. There was always something.

"Have you spoken to him about it yet?"

I shook my head. "I'll do it this weekend when he's here."

"Hey, sweetie. I have a new job."

"Really?" He was making up the single bed.

When he slept here once a month, he slept in my old room and I took the fold-out bed in the living room.

"Yep." I smiled. "Not much longer and I'll be able to afford an apartment of my own. Then you'll be able to stay much more often. I've already discussed it with your dad. He's fine with it. Maybe you can finally introduce your new girlfriend to me—if you want to."

"Which school is it?" he asked.

"Oakwood High."

His back stiffened.

"Seriously?"

He sounded just like his grandpa at breakfast.

"I promise I won't come check up on you."

He went on making the bed, straightened the bottom sheet.

He pulled it so hard that the other side came out.

"I know you have your own life, sweetie."

"Are you going to be teaching me?"

"Probably." I held my breath, waiting for his reaction.

"No way I'm going to call you Mom when we're there, if that's what you're thinking."

"You don't have to," I said quickly. "No one will know you're my son. And we have different last names, so . . ."

"It's okay." He turned to me. "Congratulations, then, I suppose."

The week after that, I started at Oakwood High.

As we'd agreed, I acted like I didn't know him.

He was just a student, like all the rest.

But after a few days, we had our first argument.

"That girlfriend of yours slashed my bike tire," I shouted at him. "That's not normal, is it?"

"You got it repaired already, didn't you?"

I couldn't believe he was so casual about it.

"That girl's no good for you, Vincent."

"My name is Vin."

"What do you see in her?"

"I just think Nova's cool."

"Even though she does things like that?"

"You shouldn't take it so personally. You get way too upset about things. I bet that's why you had all those problems at that other school too."

ALSO THAT FALL

"You talked to Reid Hunter about it?!" Vin stormed into the living room.

Dangling in his hand was the bunch of keys with the little flashlight attached.

I gave it to him on his tenth birthday. It worked on solar energy.

"I had to," I said. "That Nova of yours is making it impossible for me to teach."

"What is it this time?"

"You've seen what she does. Throwing paper, making comments about slaughtering pigs . . . It's not normal, Vin."

"That happens to every teacher at some point," Vin said, standing up for her. "Anyway, it's your own fault. She says you did something to hurt her in the past."

"What?" I stare at him in astonishment. "I don't even know the girl!"

"She says you do."

"Where from?"

"No idea."

This conversation was going in completely the wrong direction.

"And now you've sicced Reid Hunter on us!" Vin looked at me. "You even gave him my name!"

"You wanted me to treat you like an ordinary student," I reminded him.

Vin's eyes blazed at me. "Drop dead."

ALSO THAT WINTER

"Mom?" Vin came into the classroom on his own.

"What is it?" I asked in surprise.

He'd never come to talk to me at school, certainly not in my role as mother.

Vin carefully closed the door behind him.

"I . . ." I could see he was searching for the right words. "I've come to say sorry."

"What for?"

"For what happened at the supermarket. I should have stopped them. And that comment about not being able to cut the ties with Grandma and Grandpa. It wasn't fair. The divorce wasn't your fault."

I really wanted to give Vin a big hug, but I knew that he'd just crawl back into his shell.

"And you were right. Nova is . . . Nova isn't good for me."

Inside, I was cheering.

"I'm going to break up with her."

"No!" I was shocked by my own reaction, but then I continued. "You can't do that."

"Why not?"

"Because . . ." I thought about the photos.

And their part in the plan in my head that was becoming clearer and clearer.

The time was coming when I would be able to get back at them.

And with Vin at my side, that plan would be a lot easier to carry out.

"Because I need your help."

"The car's clean again." Dad came into my room. "So, those awful girls Vin hangs out with. Are you going to tell me who they are?"

"Friends of his," I said.

"Destroying your car?" Dad made a face. "I nearly had a heart attack when I saw my grandson with them!"

Vin was playing his role perfectly.

He was going along with everything, just like I'd asked him to.

The last thing I needed was for Bittersweet and Lotus to get suspicious.

"I'll talk to Vin about it," I said. "It's going to be okay."

"Do you know what she's planning now? At the dance they want to . . ."

"It doesn't matter." I shook my head. "It's nearly over."

"What do you mean? You don't want to know what she says about you, Mom. She hates you."

"I know," was all I said.

"I'm quitting." Vin clicked his flashlight on and off. "I can't do this anymore."

"No," I said. "Not yet."

Was I going to have to tell my son about the photos? But then there was a risk of everything coming out too soon. It was better if Vin didn't know that part of the story. Then, when he found out the truth, his shock wouldn't be fake.

"I can't do this anymore," Vin said again.

"Do it for me," I said. "Please."

The smell of urine stung my nose.

Vin pulled the mask off his face and looked over his shoulder.

I didn't want him to see me like this. He had to go.

"Vin," came a voice from the hallway. "Come on!"

But Vin stood there.

Another moment and he'd come over and help me to my feet. I was sure of that.

He was blinded by Bittersweet, but ultimately his loyalty was with me.

"Go on," I said in a hoarse voice.

I tried to say the rest with my eyes.

That I had a plan.

That it really would all be over soon.

He just had to wait a little longer.

Vin left.

Reid Hunter has turned on the radio, but no one is singing along.

I still don't get exactly why Mom let them go.

But as soon as the message arrived, I knew she was done.

Finally.

Maybe it was because of Nova's story about elementary school.

Could it be true?

I look to one side.

Nova's eyes meet mine and she smiles cautiously.

For a moment, I see a glimpse of the girl I got to know last year.

Before my mom came to work at our school and when everything was still normal.

When I wasn't thinking about sneaking panties back in the middle of the night.

Or hitting myself with a piece of wood to make it look as convincing as possible.

If only I could go back to that summer.

Nova, Lotus, and me.

A golden trio.

My first test came the day before yesterday.

Lotus was taking Spot out for his evening walk.

She'd been walking past Mom's new house for weeks, but of course she had no way of knowing that.

As soon as she went into the woods, Mom told me to go after her.

"Tell me the perfect moment," she had said. "And try to spook her a bit."

I put on my black hoodie and left.

Lotus wouldn't walk past me. She turned around and ran off.

I think she was terrified.

At her front door, she looked back, but she didn't see me.

I let Mom know she could begin.

It was actually me who gave the starting signal.

When Lotus read the message, she flinched.

But that was just the beginning.

* * *

I reach into my pocket.

My phone is still there.

With Mom on speed dial.

No one realized I had a phone with me too.

How many secret calls did I make to her?

That meant she could listen in on everything.

Teachers have eyes and ears everywhere.

I was her eyes and ears.

Lotus is staring out of the window. I know she's thinking about those photos she tore up.

Lotus, who has surprised me so often these past couple of days.

She was in a relationship with our teacher!

And she confessed her secret to save my skin.

Why did she do that?

Because she cares about me?

I look to one side.

Nova has fallen asleep and is snoring quietly.

When we had just started dating, I sometimes looked at her for minutes while she slept.

That's when she's at her most beautiful.

There's something soft about her.

Maybe that's how she looked before those bullies started harassing her.

She probably didn't have flames in her eyes yet.

The same flames I see in Mom's sometimes.

I carefully pull my phone from my pocket and see a new message.

Nova and Lotus have been punished enough. We're quits. I don't know who's the victim and who's the perpetrator anymore, so I'm breaking this circle. I'm letting it go. Thanks for your help, sweetie. You're the best son I could wish for.

I put my phone away and look out the window again.

I did what I had to.

But what now?

Nova asked at the farmhouse if I loved her.

I didn't reply, but what if she asks me again?

I don't know the answer.

I love her and I hate her.

I just don't know anymore.

Not much longer and we'll be home.